The Last Shinobi

The Last Shinobi

Joseph P. White

authorHOUSE®

AuthorHouse™
1663 Liberty Drive
Bloomington, IN 47403
www.authorhouse.com
Phone: 1 (800) 839-8640

Published by AuthorHouse 05/12/2015

ISBN: 978-1-5049-1204-4 (sc)
ISBN: 978-1-5049-1203-7 (e)

Library of Congress Control Number: 2015907456

Print information available on the last page.

DEDICATION

This is for my father and brother, thank you both for always believing in and having faith in me.

Also for my mother, a woman who was always a beacon of light in dark times, may your light continue to shine on our family from heaven.

PROLOUGE

There has always been a constant struggle between good and evil, light and darkness. The greatest of these struggles has been between the White Shinobi Clan and the Black Shinobi Clan. In ancient times there was a great war between these two clans, that war lasted for generations; however, on the last day of the war it seemed as though the Black Shinobi Clan had won this war; but, the last member of the White Shinobi Clan of that time made a prophecy, that in a time when evil's influence was spreading across the world the last of the White Shinobi Clan would come and bring the light and wrath of the White Shinobi Clan with him. After this prophecy was made the Black Shinobi Master, Ryan, destroyed this last remaining White Shinobi. The time of this prophecy's fulfillment is at hand, and Ryan senses that, and fearing what it means to him, he has dispatched his greatest assassins to destroy the one this prophecy speaks of.

CHAPTER ONE

THE DISCOVERING

It is present day Virginia Beach, VA, in a martial arts studio, a young man named Joseph, taking lessons in the art of the ninja and samurai sword fighting techniques, is currently engaged in a sparring match with his teacher. Joseph is a man in his mind twenties, is of average build, brown hair, brown eyes, and about six feet tall. His teacher is a black man of the same height as Joseph, but he is slimmer than Joseph with black hair and brown eyes. The two are sparing with not only fists and feet but also wooden swords. Joseph parries a slash to his midsection and carries through with the parry and turns it into a slash to his teacher's head, which his teacher deflects with an overhead block with his sword and countered it with a snap kick to Joseph's mid-section which Joseph barely avoided by jumping backwards, but then he fakes a kick which his teacher goes to block and in turn is hit by a sword slash to the midsection, which sends him back a couple of steps, and Joseph follows up with a downward slash to his teacher's head and barely misses due to his teacher's last minute dodging ability and the teacher hits Joseph with a palm strike to his chest that causes Joseph to stumble back a few feet and his teacher follows it with a low sweep which Joseph flips over and catches his teacher with a back kick which sends his teacher to the ground and Joseph follows the attacks with a stab which his teacher blocks and then sweeps Joseph off his feet and after the two get up they brace for one last sword attack and charge each other and at the last possible second slash at each other's midsection and connect at the same time. Both exhausted, remove their head gear and give each other a bow out of respect. As the two start to strip off there padding and protective gear they begin to speak.

?????- Well Joseph, your technique just gets better and better every day.

Joseph- (looking over to his instructor and nodding.) Thank you sir.

Instructor- (walking over to Joseph.) I think one day soon, you may be able to defeat me with that double sword technique of yours.

Joseph- (standing up to look in his instructor's face and also chuckling) Only time will tell sir. Well sir I have to go, I have some work to get done at home as well as some errands to take care of.

Instructor- (nodding his head) Of course Joseph. You have a good night.

Joseph- (bows to his instructor) Thank you sir, you have a good night as well.

As Joseph's instructor leaves to go in his office, Joseph finishes packing his equipment and leaves the dojo. On his way out of the dojo he passes a blonde haired woman who is going into the dojo and as she passes him she glances in his direction and nods her head to him as they pass each other. As the woman walks into the dojo, Joseph's instructor walks out of his office to finish putting his gear away.

Instructor- (as he is walking out of his office.) Excuse me miss, I'm sorry to tell you that the dojo is closed at this time.

Woman- (raising her hand to show him a mark on her hand in the shape of a dragon) Even for an old friend come to catch up.

Instructor- (taking a step back out of surprise of the mark on her hand) C-Crystal, is that really you?

Crystal- (with her hands on her hips and a devilish smile on her face) Of course it is, who else would it be?

Crystal is a woman in her early to mid-twenties, she is rather plain looking, with blonde hair that extends to just below her shoulders, blue eyes, and of average weight.

Instructor- (walking over to embrace Crystal before they speak again) It has been a long time. (motioning her into his office) Come into my office and let's talk.

As the two walk into his office she goes to a couch to sit down, while he puts on a pot of coffee.

Crystal- (looking around the office) So how have you been old friend?

Instructor- (walking over to sit next to Crystal) Well I've been as good as can be expected. Has the time come?

Crystal- (looking directly into the eyes of her old friend) Yes it has, and I know who the chosen one is. I passed him as I entered the dojo.

Instructor- (looking away from Crystal and nodding his head) I had a feeling it was him, and he doesn't know yet. (now looking down at the floor with his fingers interlaced) I'll have to tell him, he'll be back tomorrow morning, I'll tell him then.

Crystal- (placing her hand on her old friends shoulder) Good, he will believe it coming from you.

It is eight am in the morning, and the sun is shining and the grass is glittering with dew of the night before. Joseph is walking down the street carrying a black bag with his training gear in it. As he gets to the door of the studio he notices that the open sign is off; but, his instructor's vehicle is there. Joseph pulls the door open and cautiously enters the studio.

Joseph- (walking into the studio cautiously and looking around for signs of a break-in) Master, are you here?

Instructor- (walking into the room were Joseph is) I'm here Joseph, relax, nothing is wrong, I simply decided to close the studio today.

Joseph- (looking obviously confused) What? Why? I don't understand.

Instructor- (chuckling a little) I needed to talk to you and what I want to talk to you about is going to take a while, so I decided to close the studio for today rather than start the conversation over and over again. Oh and by the way don't call me sir or master anymore, instead call me Kenneth.

Joseph- (confusion in his voice) Alright mas........ I mean Kenneth. What is it you need to talk to me about?

Kenneth- (waving Joseph to follow him into his office) Tell me Joseph, have you ever heard of the legend of the White Shinobi.

Joseph- (shaking his head and sitting down in a chair) No, why?

Kenneth- (sitting in the chair behind his desk) Well because part of the legend is about you.

Joseph- (chuckling and pointing a finger at Kenneth) Funny Kenneth. From what you are saying I'm somesort of long awaited hero of a legend. If this was April 1st I'd say nice try Kenneth.

Kenneth- (his tone becoming very serious as he looks directly at Joseph) It's no joke Joseph, this legend is true. Centuries ago there were two Shinobi Clans, the White and the Black. These two clans were constantly at war with each other until one day the Black Shinobi Master of that time defeated the White Shinobi Master of that time and led his clan to the total victory over and destruction of the White Shinobi Clan. Before the last of the White Shinobi Clan was killed he made a prophecy that in a time of great darkness the very last of the White Shinobi Clan would come and avenge the White Shinobi clan. That White Shinobi he prophesized is you Joseph.

Joseph- (standing up and chilling his voice a few degrees) Kenneth, this ain't funny, enough with the bullshit, what you just told me is a legend and nothing more, there's no proof that this ever happened......

Kenneth- (raising a hand to cut Joseph off) I can prove to you that all that I say is true, (getting out of his chair and waving Joseph to follow him) come with me.

Kenneth leads Joseph into the main training room. The walls of this room show painting of different things. On one wall there is a picture of a gold dragon with several warriors in white armor underneath it, on the opposite wall there is a painting of a black dragon with warriors clad in black armor underneath it, and finally on the back wall is the picture that is Joseph's favorite, it is a ying-yang sign made out of a white dragon and a tiger. Approaching this painting Kenneth touches a part of the wall to reveal a hidden compartment in the wall that contains two twin katanas.

Kenneth- (removing the swords from there hiding place) Joseph, these are the lasts swords of the White Shinobi Clan. Only one person can unsheathe them and that is you.

Joseph- (watching Kenneth's unsuccessful attempt to unsheathe the swords and then having the swords placed in his hands) Kenneth if you can't unsheathe these swords than how am I supposed to, you are stronger than me.

Kenneth- (placing a hand on Joseph's shoulder) They will respond to your touch as the one that claims them as their one, true master.

Joseph- (his disbelief coming through in his tone) Alright I will try it, but, if I fail I don't want to hear another thing about this, understand?

Kenneth- (nodding his head) **You have my word as your master, and more importantly, as your friend.**

Joseph- (handing one of the swords to Kenneth and gripping the other by the handle and the sheathe) **Well, here goes nothing.**

After saying this Joseph successfully unsheathes the two swords one after the other, and to his amazement he feels the blades tremble in his hands. Also at this moment a woman with blonde hair extending to just blow her shoulders walk's into the room.

Joseph- (recovering from his amazement and looking at the woman) **I saw you last night as I was leaving, I take it you knew about all this?**

Crystal- (coming up to Joseph and stopping right in front of him) **Yes I did, but, I knew you wouldn't believe me if I told you, so that job fell to Kenneth** (raising a hand in Kenneth's direction) **and he did an excellent job. As for my role, I'm to help guide you to the remains of the White Shinobi Temple, were the last of the White Shinobi Armor awaits you.**

As Crystal finishes talking three figures clad in black appear in front of them from thin air.

Kenneth- (quickly turning to examine the situation) **Shit, Black Shinobi Assassins. They're here for you Joseph, somehow they found out your identity. Three of them and three of us, and one of them with a weapon, that one is yours Joseph, Crystal and I will take care of the other two.**

The two groups spread out into the different areas of the room, so as not to interfere with the others. Kenneth and his enemy move off to the left and back, while Crystal and her opponent move to the bottom of the room and right, and Joseph and his enemy stay in the dead center of the room. Kenneth and his enemy start their match with a flurry of round kicks to each other's legs, side, and head. Kenneth using his speed jumps over the round kick meant for his legs and lands just in time to block the one meant for the side of his rib cage, and manages to quickly duck one that would have taken his head off. He then retaliates with his own flurry of kicks and punches. His first attack is a round kick to his enemy's head, which his enemy ducks, but, Kenneth continues all the way around to bring his right foot to a low kick and takes his enemy off his feet; however, his enemy goes into a backwards somersault upon hitting the ground coming back up to his feet. The fight continues when Kenneth throws a straight punch for his enemy's chest which is caught and the enemy takes advantage of Kenneth's forward momentum built up from the punch to throw him to the ground against the wall. Shaking the cobwebs from his head, Kenneth sees his enemy stalking towards him. Getting his feet under himself, Kenneth launches himself into the air to come down on the Black Shinobi with a downwards punch that connects with the Black Shinobi's chest sending him back a few steps. Kenneth seeing his advantage follows up with a spinning heel kick which his enemy by pure luck manages to avoid; but, brings the kick back around in a sweep which connects and brings the Black Shinobi down to the ground rather unceremoniously. Kenneth seeing that his enemy is dazed decides to end the fight with a fist to his enemy's nose breaking it and then shoves the bone of the broken nose up into his enemy's head killing him.

Crystal squares off against her enemy parrying several kicks and punches that are coming close to her head. One of the kicks she manages to catch and uses the trapped leg of the Black Shinobi to throw him against the wall and then follows up with a thrust kick to were his head would have been had he not regained his bearing and moved at the last second. Seizing this opportunity he kicks Crystals other leg out from under her causing her to fall to the ground and as she hits, he waste no motion and climbs on top of her and starts raining punches down upon her face. Crystal, using her arms to cover herself up, uses her flexible legs and wraps them around his neck and pulls him off of her. Knowing that if he doesn't do something quick she could snap his neck, he removes her legs by bring his arms between them and pushing them apart. Both quickly realize that neither of them has an advantage on the ground and quickly get to their feet and this time it is Crystal that is on the attack. She throws a jab meant for his face which the Black Shinobi blocks, but, she follows the jab up with a hook to the temple which connects and finishes the combination up with an uppercut right below the chin, which causes him to fly backwards through the air and land on the ground on his back. Crystal seeing her opportunity, runs and leaps into the air and comes crashing down, knees first into the Black Shinobi's chest, causing his rib cage to collapse and ending this fight.

Joseph holding both of his swords in his hands is staring down his opponent who draws his two swords from their sheaths. After a few more seconds of a stare down, the two charge each other with swords swinging and clashing against one another. The Black Shinobi attacks with one sword in a vertical strike to Joseph's head. Joseph in one fluid motion swings the sword in his right hand up to block the attack and then continues it through to a horizontal slash at the Black Shinobi's stomach. The Black Shinobi realizing he wouldn't be able to get either sword up to block or parry the attack quickly jumps backwards out of range of the attack. Joseph deciding to keep up the pressure rushes in with two diagonal attacks one right after another, which the Black Shinobi barely dodges and thrusts one of his swords to stab through Joseph's heart, which Joseph manages to parry to the right with the sword in his left hand, and using the same weapon comes back with a slash across the chest which the Black Shinobi is almost able to avoid, but, receives a wound going from one side of his chest to the other. Becoming enraged by the site of his own blood the Black Shinobi rushes Joseph with a series of horizontal, vertical, and diagonal slashes that forces Joseph into a backwards motion as he attempts to block or dodge the attacks, and then the Black Shinobi slips a thrust kick to Joseph's stomach through his defenses. As a result

Joseph has the air knocked out of him and is doubled over. The Black Shinobi, seeing his opportunity, follows the thrust kick up with a powerful front kick to Joseph's face which knocks him to the ground. Upon hitting the ground one of the swords that Joseph was holding flies out of his hand, and the Black Shinobi, sensing victory, charges Joseph to finish the battle with a downward stab to his heart, but, Joseph, seeing the opening left in his opponent's attack quickly takes the sword in his right hand and brings it up to stab through his enemies heart. After this battle is over the three corpses of the Black Shinobi Assassins vanish into thin air just as they had appeared from thin air.

Joseph- (getting to his feet and breathing heavy) What…..the hell…happened to them?

Kenneth- (walking over to Joseph's side trying to catch his own breath) That is what happens when a Black Shinobi Assassin fails their mission and dies. They disappear as if they never existed.

Joseph- (now breathing normally) Great, so if they send more and we beat them we can't get any answers from them, but, if we don't we're dead.

Crystal- (joining the other two) Pretty much. After what happened here I think we should wait until tomorrow to start our search for the temple, but, we need to be careful. (turning to face Joseph and locking her eyes on his) They know who you are Joseph, and they will stop at nothing to prevent this prophecy from coming true.

Joseph- (looking at each of the other's in turn and shaking his head) Greeeeaaaaaat! So I'm the big target now, huh? Oh well, I'll see you guys tomorrow morning and you guys watch your backs alright.

Kenneth and Crystal together- (looking directly at Joseph) You too.

After this exchange Joseph picks up the two swords and sheathes them and leaves the dojo. Kenneth and Crystal get to work on straightening the dojo out and then they go into the office, each wondering what awaits them at the end of the journey to come.

CHAPTER TWO

THE FINDING OF THE WHITE SHINOBI TEMPLE

Morning has come and the grass glitters with the morning dew. The three, Joseph, Kenneth, and Crystal meet outside the dojo. All three are wearing their normal street clothes which allow them a range of motion for fighting should the need arise. Joseph is also carrying his black bag; but, instead of the normal training gear that is usually in it, it contains his two swords. As the three approach each other Joseph notices that both Kenneth and Crystal a holding torn sheets of paper.

Joseph- (stopping in front of Kenneth and Crystal and looking at each in turn) Good morning guys. (now looking down at the two sheets of torn paper) What are those?

Crystal- (looking Joseph in the eye and holding up the piece of paper she has) Both Kenneth and myself have been keeping hold of a map. We decided long ago that to protect the location of the temple from the Black Shinobi we should separate the map into two pieces until the chosen one arrived.

Joseph- (taking a better look at the sheets of paper) I don't see any indications of any type of map on these, what's going on?

Kenneth- (looks at Joseph) The map has to be put back together in order for it to appear, and the only one capable of doing that is you.

After hearing this Joseph places his bag on the ground and takes the two sheets of paper from Kenneth and Crystal, and holding them up before himself carefully fits the two pieces back together. As the two pieces become one you can see a light shining along the line were the map had been torn in two.

Joseph- (eye's wide in amazement) Well that was interesting. Now if I'm reading this right it says we have to go under ground. (letting out a breath) Great, we have to go into the sewer for the first part of our trip.

Kenneth- (shaking his head) I was hoping to avoid having to do that.

Crystal- (looking at the two of them) Well it's a dirty job, but somebody's gotta do it.

Joseph bends over to pick up his bag with the two swords and the three head to the nearest manhole cover and begin the decent into the sewer. When the three reach the bottom of the ladder Joseph pulls his swords from his bag and places them on his back. Kenneth pulls a small flashlight from his pocket and hands it to Joseph. Turning the flash light on Joseph notices a change in the map.

Joseph- (pointing the flashlight at Kenneth) Hey what is going on with the map, there a two arrows on it and one is blinking.

Kenneth- (coming up beside Joseph and looking at the map) I think the one arrow that is blinking is us while the other is the direction we want to go.

Joseph- (turning his attention back to the map) Alright then, let's get moving.

Crystal -(stopping the other two before the get to far) Hold on a minute, I have something else that might help us (she pulls out what looks to be a compass). I realize the likely hood of us running into Black Shinobis down here are very slim, but, we all know that there are other types of dangers down here as too, hopefully this will help us avoid or at least be prepared for those dangers.

Kenneth- (looking at Crystal with amusement)How is a compass going to help us in that area.

Crystal- (handing the compass to Joseph) You will see soon enough.

As Joseph places the compass near the map he sees that the map again goes through a change. In areas that had been blank on the route they were to take, there are now red "x's" in some of the areas.

Joseph- (looking up at Crystal) I take it the places marked with an "x" are places we want to avoid if we can.

Crystal merely nods and the three move out. As the map leads them through an underground sewer maze to their next leg of the journey, they manage, with a little luck and good timing to avoid most of the dangers in the sewer, with the exception of a few random encounters which they get past with relative ease. As the three come to the end of their journey in the sewer, they find that the next leg of their journey is through a forest. As the three begin their travel through the forest, Joseph notices a sign.

Joseph- (looking at the sign) Hey guys over here.

Kenneth and Crystal rush to Joseph's side and examine the sign he has found. The sign reads: **those who are foolish enough to travel through this forest will learn the true meaning of the phrase pain and suffering. Once you enter this forest you can only leave through the other end, if you don't have the courage needed for this, leave now, for if you don't you shell die.**

Kenneth- (shaking his head) Why do places like this forest always have to have something that always tells of doom.

Crystal- (looking into the forest and seeing a skeleton and pointing it out for the other two to see it as well) I don't know; but, I think this forest lives up to the reputation it has. Joseph is there any way around this forest.

Joseph- (looking at the map and studying it for a couple of minutes before answering) It doesn't look like it, one way leads to a mountain, that doesn't look claimable, and the other leads to a river which we don't have the equipment to cross. It looks like we have to go through this forest.

Kenneth- (shrugging his shoulders) Well no one said this was going to be easy. Let's go.

The three of them enter the forest and start making their way through it. As the three continue their travel they see numerous skeletons, and at some areas spots of dried blood on tree trunks. Three hours through their journey they hear a monstrous cry and in the distance see a shadow move faster than their eyes can track.

Crystal- (looking around to try to spot the creature again) What the hell was that?

Joseph- (looking around as well) I have no idea, but I don't think we should stop moving. Lets get going.

The three start moving again, and after another two hours of traveling through the skeleton laden forest they can see the end.

Kenneth- (pointing to the opening in the forest)Alright we made it.

Voice- (a deep inhuman voice) Not yet you haven't!!!!!!! HAHAHAHAHAHAHA!!!!!!! TO GET OUT YOU MUST DEFEAT US!!!!!!!!!!

Joseph, Kenneth, and Crystal start looking around the area trying to find the source of the voice they had just heard, and then to their left a creature that looks like a minatar leaps from the top of the tallest tree in that area. This minatar is carrying a large battle ax, a sword, and a throwing knife. From behind the three warriors a creature that looks to be a combination of part tree and part human comes out of nowhere. This creature has the shape of a human, but has what can only look like tree bark in place of skin.

Minator- (looking at each warrior in turn) To get out of this forest to the area beyond, one of you will have to fight both of us, and win. If you lose, well needless to say you lose more than the fight. Hahahaha!!!!

Creature- (moving forward) The only thing is you don't chose who fights, we do.

Joseph- (cautionously stepping forward) What are you two, demons?

Minator- (looking him in the eye) No, we were once men like you, but, one day we ran across what we thought was a dying creature (starting to pace the area), you can imagine our surprise when it turned out to be some sort of spirit that had decided to play a game. It turned us into these creatures you see before you know, and made it so that we could never leave this forest until the day we died, unfortunately we can't let someone kill us, they have to do that on their own. We have been alive for over two hundred years. But enough of this it is time to fight and you (pointing at Joseph) will be the one to fight us.

Joseph- (unsheathing his swords) Very well, I hope this will be the last time you have to fight.

The minatar charges Joseph swinging his battle ax at Joseph's midsection, while the other creature sinks into the ground to prepare for his attack, meanwhile, Joseph flips over the minatars strike with the battle ax and in return as he lands, he is able to catch the minatar with a downward slash from the sword in his right hand. The creature that sank into the ground comes up out of the ground behind Joseph and wraps him in vines. The minatar turns to see that Joseph his been trapped by his friend, and tossing his ax from one hand to the other, walks over to Joseph and attacks with a downward slash, Joseph, at the last second turns his body and the attack meant to split him in half frees him the vines that his other opponent wrapped him in. Joseph leaps back out of their reach and into a tree. The minatar, with an insane look in his eyes, charges towards the tree that Joseph is in and leaps into it, while his friend again sinks into the ground. In the tree, the minatar and Joseph are fighting a fierce battle. The minatar tries to land a horizontal slash to Joseph's stomach which Joseph blocks with the sword in his right hand and then retailiates with a diagonal slash from the upper left to the lower right to the minatar. Quickly taking out his throwing knife the minator blocks Joseph's slash, and out of nowhere, the minator's friend's hands grab Joseph by his feet. Joseph seeing that his chances of winning are going down the drain decides to take a wreckless chance and slashes through the branch he is on starting a plummet to the ground. The creature that grabbed Joseph's legs let's go of them and is seen leaping from the branch to the safety of a nearby tree. Seeing an opportunity to take out one of the creatures he has to fight, he leaps from the plummeting branch to the tree the branch was attached to and pushing off the side of that tree, sours to the tree that the minator's friend is in and just as he starts sinking into the tree, Joseph, with both swords, slashes through the creature's stomach with one blade and with the other, takes off the head. The creature starts to turn to dust. The minator enraged at seeing his friend killed in battle sends his throwing knife through the air and follows it towards Joseph. Joseph leaps from the branch he was standing on to another tree to avoid the throwing knife and the oncoming minator. Seeing an opportunity to take the fight back to the ground Joseph leaps from the tree he just landed on and connects with a thunderous flying side kick to the side of the head of the minator sending him hurtling to the ground. Upon impact with the ground the battle ax that the minator was using flies out of his hands and lodges itself into a tree. Joseph leaping from the tree goes flying to the ground feet first, intending to drive his feet through the minator. The minator, seeing this, roll's out of the way as Joseph lands with a thunderous thud on the ground. The minator, getting to his feet quickly, charges Joseph from behind and sends him flying into a tree head first and then bouncing off the tree and landing on ground on his back. Getting up slowly, Joseph sees that the minator has abandoned his ax for his sword and is charging him with it. The minator, as he nears Joseph, does a horizontal slash that Joseph leaps over. After Joseph lands on his feet, he throws a roundhouse kick with his foot and catches the minator on the right side of his head, dazing him for a few seconds. Joseph, seeing that the mintor is dazed attacks with a double horizontal slash from left to right opening the minator's stomach. The minator leaping back away from Joseph examines his wounds and looks at Joseph with what can only be assumed to be a smile. The minator, now with a business look on his face, charges Joseph swinging his sword wildly. As he nears Joseph, he leaps over him and while Joseph is in mid-air, the minator turns so that he is facing Joseph's back and as Joseph lands, the minator does a diagonal slash to Joseph's back from left to right. In an effort to avoid the attack Joseph attempts to roll out of the way from the minator's sword; however, the minator's sword connects with Joseph's back. Joseph, ignoring the pain from his wound, rolls back to his feet, turns, and charges the minator and the minator charges Joseph at the same time. The minator, with both hands on the hilt of his sword, does a horizontal slash from right to left that Joseph leaps over and comes down behind the minator and as he lands he turns slashing one blade from right to left of the minator and using the other sword does a downward slash. As Joseph turns to walk to his friends the minator is seen dropping to the ground in four pieces.

Joseph- (as he reaches Kenneth and Crystal and sheathing his swords) This battle is over, let's go.

As the three turn and start to leave the spirits of the two creatures appear as men in front of them.

The one that was once the minator- (looking at Joseph and bowing his head) We thank you for setting us free from our curse. Now we want to repay you.

The spirit of the man that was once the minator raises his hand and the map that Joseph was carrying floats into the air and starts to glow and a new location and path appear on the map.

The spirit of the man that once had tree bark for skin-(lifting his head and looking at each of the three warriors in turn)The place that is marked is the temple that you are looking for, and the path is as far as we know the safest path to the temple. (now looking at Joseph and raising a hand that emit a glowing light that heals Joseph's wound) Again we thank you for freeing us from our curse, and we hope you accomplish what you have set out to do, and for us we can now join our families in the afterlife.

The two spirits disappear and the three warriors head out on the new path to the location of the White Shinobi Temple. As the warriors travel the new path that had been marked on their map, they discover that the path truely is safe, and aside from a few inconviences they make it to the temple without a single incidence.

Kenneth- (placing a hand on Joseph's shoulder) From this point on you must go alone, only you as the master of the White Shinobi Clan will be granted access into the temple.

Joseph- (looking at both Kenneth and Crystal in turn) I understand. Do either of you have any idea of what I will be facing in there?

Crystal- (coming up beside Kenneth) I'm afriad that all we know is that you will be tested in three different ways, what those tests are we don't know.

Joseph- (turning to begin walking to the temple entrance) Alright, I'll be back as soon as I can.

As Joseph starts walking up to the temple a door opens in front of him and he walks through it not knowing how he will be tested.

Crystal- (silently to herself as Kenneth moves away from her) Good like and may you return safely and swiftly.

CHAPTER THREE

THE WHITE SHINOBI TEMPLE AND THE CHALLENGES OF A SHINOBI MASTER

As Joseph makes his way into the temple he finds himself walking down a hall that has giant stone statues of the past masters of the White Shinobi Clan. As he moves further into the temple, certain areas begin to illuminate as he enters them, and as he reaches the furthest area, he is greeted by a mysterious voice.

Voice- Who has entered this sacred place? Speak now or prepare to die.

Joseph- (spinning around and looking for the source of the voice) My name is Joseph, I am the one that the prophecy speaks of. I have come to claim the armor and power's that I will need to face this great evil that takes the form of the Black Shinobi Master.

Voice- (growing less aggressive) Very well young one; but, in order to obtain this armor and power you speak of you must undergo three tests, are you prepared to do so?

Joseph- (giving up on finding the location of the voice and answering without any hesitation) Yes, I am. Let them begin

Voice- As you wish. Your first test is to walk through a wall of flames.

Before Joseph can say anything, a giant wall of flames appears before him, and as he looks at it, the confusion can be seen on his face.

Joseph- (with confusion in his voice) I don't understand what this test has to do with me obtaining the armor and power I need to have to fight this evil.

Voice- These flames have two purposes. The first is to be a test of the purity of your heart and soul, for only one with a pure heart and soul can you truly be called a White Shinobi Master and obtain the power needed to defeat the Black Shinobi Master and his clan. The second purpose is to connect you with the element that is in your heart, the element of fire. Every White Shinobi Master has had a connection with some sort of element of this world whether it is of water, earth, wind, light, or in your case, fire. To pass this test you must walk through these flames and come out on the other side without so much as a single burn.

Joseph- (clenching his fist in preparation) I understand.

Joseph now with the understanding of why this test is needed begins his walk through the flames, and even though the flames lick at his body and burn holes in his clothing, Joseph comes out on the other side without a single burn on him.

Voice- (with amazement in his voice) Very well done young one, now you must prepare for the second test.

Joseph- (looking at his body with amazement and then turning his attention to the voice) What does the second test consist of?

Voice- So you are ready. In the second test you must fight and defeat three enemies without the use of a weapon or your sight.

Joseph- (looking discouraged and with nervousness in his voice) If I was just fighting without the use of weapons I wouldn't have a problem with it; but, how am I supposed to fight something I can't see?

Voice- (with an admonishing tone) Are you truly that unsure of your other senses? Your senses of hearing, touch, smell, and in some cases taste can more than make up for the loose of one sense, you must learn to use them. There is also what some people term as a sixth sense or as I call it a danger sense. It is a feeling you get when something bad is about to happen. The purpose of this test is to get you more attuned to all those senses. Now prepare to defend yourself.

A bolt of lightning strikes the ground in front of Joseph, causing him to temporarily go blind, and three more strike the ground causing three warriors to appear, one on either side, and one behind Joseph. The three warriors waste no time in attacking Joseph. The warrior to Joseph's back attacks him with an elbow thrust to his lower back, while the other two warriors attack simultaneously, one kicking him in his chest and one sweeping the legs out from under him. As Joseph hits the ground on his back he rolls into a backwards somersault, and attempting to catch the one behind him with an attack, he thrust his feet straight up and connects with that one under his chin, sending him into the air. As Joseph gets to his feet he receives a punch to his chest, but, ignoring the pain from the attack, grabs the arm of his attacker and breaks it by pushing the upper portion of the arm to the inside, and the lower portion of the arm to the outside, then he lets go of the now broken arm of the attacker and lands a combo of a left jab, right hook, a thrust kick to double his attacker over, and finally a mighty uppercut to send his opponent crashing to the ground in an unconscious heap. As his defeated foe hits the ground, Joseph hears the warrior that had attacked him from behind, get to his feet and charge him. As the warrior nears Joseph, the warrior leaps into the air and attempts to land a flying side kick, which Joseph avoids by spinning his body to the right and the as the warrior starts to fly past him he strikes him with a horizontal chop to the warriors back knocking him to the ground. Joseph then walks over to the place the warrior landed and stomps his right foot down on the neck of the warrior with the force needed to break his neck. As Joseph takes his foot off the broken neck of the fallen warrior, he feels the air being displaced by a sword moving towards his head. Joseph quickly jumps back away from the incoming blade, and feels several more attacks coming from it that he dodges. Joseph knowing that he has to wait for the right time to attack. Sensing a horizontal slash to his midsection coming, Joseph moves in to catch his attacker's hand in a spinning motion and during this motion, removes the sword from his attacker and then continuing around, using the sword to remove his attacker's head. As the head of the attacker starts to roll off his body, the bodies of the three defeated warrior's disappear as well as the sword in Joseph's hands. In a third flash of lightning Joseph's vision is restored.

Voice- Well done, not many Shinobi have been able to recover that quickly from loosing there sight to fight as efficiently as you did. You did very well indeed.

Joseph- (catching his breathe) Thank you, what is the third test?

Voice- (with amusement in it's voice) You are indeed showing why you are the one that was chosen to be a Shinobi Master. Your third and final test is this, you must make your way through a maze to its center, and there face your worst fear. A White Shinobi cannot be afraid of something so much that it causes him to stop doing that which must be done, the purpose of this test is to make you face the thing you fear the most and overcome it to prove that no fear will ever stop you in accomplishing your mission.

Joseph- (closing his eyes and nodding his head) I understand.

From the ground, a giant maze rises up, and before Joseph enters it he takes one last deep breathe. As Joseph enters the maze he finds that there is no marked path and as he attempts to go to the center he finds himself doubling back many times from taking wrong turns. Two hours into his journey he finally makes it to the center of the maze, and from the other side a man walks out that looks just like Joseph in every respect except instead of brown eyes he has blood-red eyes.

Joseph- (with understanding in his voice) So, if I'm right the thing I have always feared the most is my dark side and sense you are here, that means I have to face and defeat you.

Evil Joseph- (laughing mockingly) You think you can defeat me, huh, go ahead and try, but, should you fail, I am set free from you for all eternity.

Joseph- (getting into his fighting stance and speaking with determination in his voice) That will never happen.

The battle between Joseph and his evil counter-part begins. Both are evenly matched. Joseph lands a thrust punch to the stomach of his evil counter-part, who takes the attack and sends a roundhouse kick of his own to Joseph's head, which causes Joseph to stumble back a few feet. The evil counter-part seeing an opportunity follows his attack with a side kick that Joseph catches and as he catches the leg of his evil counter-part he starts a spinning motion and uses the momentum to hurl his evil counter-part against one of the walls of the giant maze. Joseph, seeing his advantage, charges his evil counter-part and attacks with a punch that barely misses and connects with the wall causing the area were his fist hit to crack. Seeing an opportunity for attack, the evil counter-part charges Joseph, but, Joseph was ready for something such as this and thrust his elbow into his counter-parts face, causing him to stumble back a few steps. The battle goes on like this for two hours with niether gaining or losing ground.

Evil Joseph- (breathing heavy and frustration in his voice) Why can't I beat you? I don't understand it.

Joseph- (breathing heavy and having a moment of clarity) I think I understand. You are my worst fear, that means you will always be a part of me and I can't kill you anymore than I can kill myself. I have to accept this truth.

Evil Joseph- (full of rage in his voice) That's not true, I'll kill you now. AAAAAAAAAAAAAARRRRRRRRR RRRRRR!!!!!!!!!!!!!!!!!!!!!

As the evil counter-part charges to strike, Joseph prepares himself. The evil counter-part attacks first with a jab with the left hand, which is blocked, and then a hook with the right hand which is also blocked, and Joseph now on the inside of his evil counter-part's guard, embraces him and as he does so the maze and his evil counter-part disappear. As this happens the voice reveals itself and its shape is that of the golden dragon that Joseph saw on the painting on the wall at Kenneth's dojo.

Dragon- (with a smile on his face) Well done White Shinobi Master. You realized that you couldn't kill your fear only accept and overcome it. Now you are ready to receive the armor and powers that are rightfully yours.

After the Dragon says this he engulfs Joseph in his flames, and as the flames die down, Joseph emerges from them in a suit of glowing armor. The sleeves and leggings of are a reddish-orange color, as is the top of the helmet. On either side of the helmet, there is a metallic horn and the face mask is gray. The armor of the shoulders, chest and abdomen is a white color, that has a golden dragon emblazoned on the chest piece.

Joseph- (looking at the armor in wide-eyed amazement) I can't believe this, I've never felt anything like this before.

Dragon- (chuckling at Joseph) Yes, the power you now have is great; however, you cannot defeat the Black Shinobi Master alone. One of the abilities you now possess is to make White Shinobi Warriors of those that you deem worthy, and there are at least two that are waiting for you now; but, before you go I most share some of my knowledge with you.

Joseph- (looking up at the dragon in confusion as well as lifting his hands in a jesture of confusion to just above his waist) What else is there that I need to know?

Dragon- (with a calm tone in his voice) You must know the origin of the prophecy that you are a part of. I'm sure you have wondered why you are the one that was chosen to become the White Shinobi Master, the truth is that you are a descendant of the last Master of the White Shinobi Clan. Before that fateful day of the clan's destruction at the hands of the Black Shinobi Master, Ryan, your ancestor's first wife became pregnant. Because of the state of war that the clan was in, any woman, including the master's wife, was sent to a secret place to go through the pregnancy and give birth. Shortly after your ancestor's wife was sent to this place, the clan was attacked and destroyed, at least that is what Ryan thought. You as of right now are all that remains of the White Shinobi Clan; until, you make White Shinobi Warriors of those that are worthy. Be aware that when you leave this place, the Virginia you know will not exist. Your influence out in that world kept the darkness of the Black Shinobi in check and kept it from spreading, that influence was taken away once you came in here, because this is a completely different dimension from the one that you are from, and with your influence missing, the influence of the Black Shinobi is spreading. By now it would have taken over most of what you call Virginia; however, you should return in time to stop that influence from spreading all over the world.

Joseph- (clenching his fists at his side)I understand,(relaxing his hands by unclenching his fists and looking directly into the dragon's eyes) tell me, how do I make Kenneth and Crystal into White Shinobi Warriors?

Dragon- (looking into Joseph's eyes as well; but, still speaking in a calm voice) The answer to that question is very simple. First, you must be as you are now, and second, you must touch each of them on their shoulders with the blades you now carry on your back. This is how you will make anyone worthy of being a White Shinobi Warrior into one. The time has come for you to depart this place and fulfill your destiny. I wish you luck.

CHAPTER FOUR

THE BEGINNINGS OF THE NEW CLAN AND THE BEGINNING OF A NEW JOURNEY.

As Joseph leaves the White Shinobi Temple he makes his way back to where his comrades are waiting for him.

Joseph- (stopping in front of his friends and looking each of them in the eye in turn) Well as you guys can see, I succeeded, (drawing his swords) the two of you have more than proven yourselves as friends and allies and I would be honored if the two of you would become the first two members of the new White Shinobi Clan.

Kenneth and Crystal- (bowing their heads and speaking at the same time) It is us who are honored.

With each sword Joseph touches first Kenneth and then Crystal on each shoulder. As he removes the blades from their shoulders the two warriors are engulfed in flames similar to those that Joseph himself was engulfed in. As the flames around them die down they emerge in their armor. Kenneth's armor, like Joseph's is white, however, his weapon, instead of a sword it is a three sectional staff. Like Joseph's and Kenneth's armor, Crystal's is also white, and her weapon is a golden bow and arrow set that never runs out of arrows. The main similarity of all these armors is that they all have golden dragons on the chest plate.

Joseph- (Sheathing his swords) It is time to head back, and bring an end to the evil that Ryan stands for.

The three warriors head back to where their journey began only to see as the emerge from the sewer that Virginia Beach has changed. Very few, if any, buildings are left standing, the water in the area is black, the once blue sky is eternally covered by a cloud of thick smoke, and the most noticeable of the changes is a giant mountain range that has an active volcano in it.

Crystal- (looking around in disbelief) What happened here?

Joseph- (looking around and clenching his fists) The dragon told me that this would happen, I didn't want to believe him though, it's the influence of the Black Shinobi Clan. I was the only thing keeping it in check, and when I left to obtain the armor and powers I now have (pausing briefly and looking down) there was nothing stopping that influence. (looking up with a new resolve in his eyes) I have to set things right, and the only way to do that is to destroy Ryan. Let's get moving.

Joseph and Crystal start to leave, but, before they get to far ahead Kenneth stops them.

Kenneth- (grabbing Joseph by the arm) We're not ready for this journey yet. We have no idea what we'll come across out there. I'm pretty sure that the water is to polluted to drink even if we do boil it first, we need to find a place where we can get some supplies before we leave.

Joseph- (looking at his long time teacher and friend) Your right. Let's split up and meet back here in an hour. Get anything you think we can use, bottled water, food that won't spoil, climbing gear, and so on. Both of you be careful.

As the three split to go on their quest for supplies, it is unknown to them that they are being watched from the ruins of what was once Kenneth's martial arts studio.

Hooded figure 1- (turning to the other hooded figure next to him) Go to the master, and tell him that our enemy has finally emerged, he will be pleased with us.

Hooded figure 2- (nodding his head in agreement) Yes very pleased he will be, but, what will you be doing while this one informs the master?

Hooded figure 1- (looking in the direction that Kenneth is taking) This one will follow that one (pointing at Kenneth) and wait for the right time to strike.

Hooded figure 2- (nodding his head in approval) Yes, a very good plan, I wish you success brother.

The two hooded figures leave the martial arts studio, one following Kenneth in the shadows, while the other heads back to his master to report on the news that his enemies have reappeared.

Hooded figure 2- (bowing in front of a man in black armor sitting on a throne) Master, this one reports that he has seen the master's enemies re-emerge.

Master- (standing from his throne and looking down at his underling) You have done well to report this to me(lifting a finger to propose a question), however, I seem to remember sending two of you, tell me where is your brother?

Hooded figure 2- (responding with a trembling voice) Ma….. Ma…..Master, this one's brother went to set an ambush for one of this one's Master's enemies.

Master- (with an evil smile coming to his lips) Well I hope for your sake he succeeds, cause you know what awaits you if he fails, you will share his fate. HAHAHAHAHAHAHAHAHahahahahahhaahha!!!!!!!!!!!!!!

Meanwhile the other hooded figure follows Kenneth on his errand waiting for the right time to strike. Kenneth has gone to the remains of a quick mart in the hopes of finding some of the supplies, such as pure water and food. To his amazement he does find some bottled water and food that he can take back to the others. He put them in a backpack he managed to find along the way at an abandoned sports store along with some climbing gear. As he finishes packing the food and water, he hears the terrified scream of a woman in trouble and heads in the direction of the scream to check it out. As he nears the area of the screams he finds that two Black Shinobi assassins and rushes to her aid. The two assassins upon seeing Kenneth turn their attention towards him. Meanwhile one hour has passed and Joseph and Crystal have met up outside of the ruins of Kenneth's martial arts studio.

Joseph- (looking around to see if he can spot Kenneth coming) This isn't like Kenneth. He's never late, especially when it's something of this importance.

Crystal- (with confidence in her voice) Don't worry about Kenneth, he can take care of himself.

Joseph- (still looking around and with concern in his voice) I don't know Crystal, I just have a bad feeling about something. I hope it's nothing though.

After a few minutes more the two look at each other and nod in silent agreement to go look for their lost friend. The two travel to an area five minutes away and discover that Kenneth is protecting a young girl about Joseph's age from two Black Shinobi assassins and to make matters worse he has sustained an injury during the fight. The two rush to Kenneth's aid to join the fight.

Crystal attacks the assassin on the right side of Kenneth with a stunning roundhouse kick that knocks him to the ground. She wastes no motion, leaping into the air to come straight down like a bolt of lightning on his chest crushing his ribs and he dies and vanishes underneath her. Joseph attacks the assassin on Kenneth's left side. He starts the fight out with a quick combination to the face of the assassin that consists of a jab with his left fist, a hook punch with his right, and finally an upper-cut with his left that sends his opponent back a couple of steps. Recovering quickly, the assassin retaliates with a combination of his own of a jab, which Joseph blocks, a hook, which connects to the side of Joseph's head, and a roundhouse kick that sends Joseph to the ground. Shaking the cobwebs out of his head, Joseph regains his footing and goes back on the attack., first, with a knee shattering forward thrust kick to the assassins right leg, followed by a nose breaking thrust punch, and ends it with a neck breaking roundhouse kick that kills the assassin and Joseph stands there watching him disappear into nothingness.

Even in his weakened state, Kenneth, senses a sneak attack coming from above and manages to push the girl out of harm's way while dodging what would have been a killing blow with a nasty looking knife. Taking a couple of seconds to size up this new comer, Kenneth decides that he is not a Black Shinobi assassin, but, a want to be assassin waiting for the right moment to strike. Even weakened Kenneth has no choice but to fight this new comer or die. The would be assassin attacks with a slash from left to right at Kenneth's midsection, an attack that Kenneth is able to block, and he makes his attacker pay for his mistake of underestimating him by breaking his arm at the elbow, then seeing the opportunity to end it quickly, Kenneth moves to behind his attacker in one, quick, flowing motion, and snipes his neck, and the would be assassin falls to the ground. Shortly after the would be assassin falls, Kenneth falls to the ground growing weaker from his injuries. As Joseph is checking on the woman that Kenneth was protecting, Crystal goes to aid Kenneth in whatever way she can.

Joseph- (looking the young woman in the eyes) Are you okay miss….?

Woman- (cutting Joseph off) My name is Kim, and yes I'm fine. Who are you…….(being cut off by Crystal)

Crystal- (panic in her voice) Joseph, Kenneth has a pretty bad wound here, I can't stop the bleeding.

As soon as Joseph hears this he rushes to his friend's side. Upon arriving he places his hands on top of one another and then on top of Kenneth's wound and a glowing, white light is admitted from under his hands and Kenneth's wound is healed.

Kim- (looking on in stunned amazement) Who are you guys, (turning to Joseph) and how did you just do that?

Joseph- (showing how weak the ability he just used made him by panting) My name is Joseph, (pointing to the others in turn as he introduces them) and this is Kenneth, who just saved your life, and Crystal. As for how I just did that, I'm not even sure myself, I acted on instinct, and as you can see, it left me a little weak. Now it's my turn to ask you a question, Kim was it, what did those Black Shinobi Assassins want with you?

Kim- (looking at the warriors with an air of caution) Yes Kim is my name, as for what those creeps wanted with me, I was supposed to become Ryan's wife, but I refused, so he had my village burned to the ground, and only allowed me to live so I could watch everyone else die, and then he was going to force me to become his wife or kill me, which I don't know.

Kenneth- (getting off the ground and looking Kim in the eyes) I'm glad I was able to help you, but for now, I think it would be best if you found somewhere to hide until all of this has ended.

Kim- (with a curious tune in her voice) What do you mean, until all this has ended?

Joseph- (letting out a sigh and looking at Kenneth first) My friend, sometimes you say too much. (looking and speaking to Kim now) He means that we are on our way to fight Ryan and bring an end to his evil.

Kim- (wide eyed, and disbelief in her voice) That is impossible, he is the strongest of the Black Shinobi Clan, there is a reason why he is its master.

Joseph- (shaking his head) And there is a reason why I am the master of the White Shinobi Clan.

Kim is stunned into silence at this point and the three warriors take this opportunity to gather their things and head out, on the path that leads to the valley of the volcano, however, as they leave Joseph calls back a few last words to Kim.

Joseph- (calling over his shoulder as they leave) I suggest you do as my friend here said, find a place to lay low. This will all be over within several days one way or the other.

As the three warriors disappear and Kim is left standing in the ruins where she was attacked, she makes a decision to follow them, to learn more about them, and maybe to try and join their quest for her own reasons. As the three travel late into the day, with Kim far enough behind them that they can't see her, Joseph finds his thoughts going back to Kim during their travels.

Joseph- Hey, do you guys think we should have left Kim like that?

Crystal- (a teasing tone in her voice) Ahhh, are you worried about her, or is it that you have a little crush on her(giggling)?

Joseph- (face turning a little red, but, tries to play it off) I'm just worried about her, I mean the assassins were after her when you showed up there Kenneth, who knows what could of happened to her after we left.

Kenneth- (accusing tone in his voice) Just worried about her huh?

Joseph- Yeah, why?

Kenneth- (teasing) Then why is your face all red all of a sudden.

Joseph- (stumbling over his words) What are you talking about, my face isn't ah red, I can't be.

Crystal- (laughing as she talks) Sure whatever you say. Hehehehe

As Crystal is laughing at Joseph's bad attempt to cover up his attraction to Kim, Joseph, hears something behind them and stops the other two, happy that he can change the subject and maybe get away from them for a couple of minutes.

Joseph- (stopping in his tracks and listening intently to something) **Did you guys hear that?**

Kenneth- (thinking that Joseph is trying to change the subject but willing to listen) **Hear what Joseph.**

Joseph- I think someone or something might be following us, you two stay here, I'm gonna double back and check it out.

With that, Joseph sprints into the high grass to get concealment for himself as he doubles back to check and see if anyone is following them. After about five minutes of heading back the way they came from, Joseph sees a figure moving through the grass just as he is and attempts to come up behind the figure in a small clearing that it is heading for. As he moves to the clearing, careful not to make a lot of noise, he circles around his quarry and discovers that the person tracking him and his comrades is Kim.

Joseph- (stepping out of the grass and into the open field behind Kim) **Why are you following us?**

Kim- (startled by the voice coming from behind her, she moves forward and turns into a defensive posture until she sees that it is Joseph) **How did you know I was following you?**

Joseph- (placing his hands on his hips) **That is none of your concern, now I'll ask again, why are you following us.**

Kim- (stepping forward just a little) I wanted to learn more about you and your friends and maybe even join your group.

Joseph- (shaking his head) **Your wasting your time.**

Kim- I don't think so, if you guys are gonna go up against Ryan, your gonna need all the help you can get.

Joseph- (letting out a sigh) **Why do you want to come so badly?**

Kim- (sadness in her voice) He had everyone in my village killed, (now anger in her voice) I want his head on a silver platter.

Joseph- I appreciate your honesty, but, your reasons are vengeance, I can't let you join us with those reasons. (pointing back the way she came) Get outta here, your better off hiding and waiting for this to be ended by us.

Kim- You can tell me to go back all you want but I'm still going to follow you.

Joseph- (sighing and seeing that there is nothing he can do to change her mind) IF, I let you join us, it's under the condition that you do what I tell you when I tell you, understand, and this is non-negotiable.

Kim- I understand, and I agree.

Joseph- Well then, I guess I should get you prepared. (spreading his legs shoulder width apart and crossing his arms across his chest) FLAMES OF SHINOBI, IGNITE!!!!!!!!!!!!!!!!!!!!!

Upon calling out this command, Joseph's body is engulfed in white flames. As Kim witnesses this, her eyes light up in terror until the flames die down and Joseph emerges in his white armor, then her expression changes to one of ah.

Joseph- (stepping towards Kim) Well, I guess I should get you suited up, (drawing his swords) take a knee.

Kim, remembering the agreement she had with him does as he orders, and as her knee touches the ground Joseph touches her on the shoulders with his blades, and much the same as Joseph was she is engulfed in flames and when they die down she emerges in the female counterpart of Joseph's armor, and as with the others, on her chest plate there is an emblem of a golden dragon, however, she notices that the one thing that sets her armor apart in appearance from his is that the dragon on his chest plate is more detailed. Unfortunately, she does not have the time to study the designs more closely because upon the end of her transformation, Joseph and she are attacked by four Black Shinobi Warriors. As the battle begins, Joseph and Kim split up, each taking on two opponents.

Kim starts the battle off on the defensive side. While parrying multiple sword slashes, she also manages to dodge a series of chain whip attacks from one of her enemies. The warrior with the chain whip also attacks with a sickle. He attacks her with it in a downwards motion that she catches on one of her blades just above her head, whiles blocking a horizontal attack with the other blade at the same time from her other enemy. With both of their weapons blocked, the nod in unison, and they use a thrust kick to her midsection at the same time that frees their weapons and sends Kim to the ground. Seeing her disadvantage, Kim quickly gets to her feet and attacks with a series of horizontal slashes at each of their midsections and vertical slashes going from one shoulder to the opposite hip; however, having to divide her attention between the two Black Shinobi Warriors is lessening the effectiveness of her attacks which in turn causes each of her attacks to be blocked by her enemies. Seeing that her best chance of winning this battle lies in separating her two opponents she leaps into a tree and starts to bound from one tree to another. The two warriors follow her into the shadows of the trees and one manages to get ahead of the other, and catching up to Kim starts the battle in the trees. While perched cautiously on a branch Kim awaits the nearer of the two warriors and as he approaches she attacks. She manages to catch him off guard with a flurry of lightning fast kicks to the legs, stomach, chest, and head, causing him to lose his balance and fall from the tree. As the second of the two warriors nears her position she decides that the best action is to start moving in the opposite direction again to put some distance between the two of them so she can set up for another attack, one she hopes will end this warriors life. As she starts moving she starts to look for an area where she can hide and spring a trap, and in the top of an old tree she spots the perfect hiding place and heads directly for it. Getting into position, just in time to see her second enemy pass by her position, she waits until he is a good ten seconds past her, then she climbs down and charges him full speed with both blades drawn and again attacks with a flurry of horizontal and vertical strikes. Caught off guard by this attack the Black Shinobi Warrior is unable to mount a solid defense and several of the attacks strike him in his chest, stomach, arms and legs, leaving his movements sluggish and predictable. Seeing her chance to take one of her enemies out, Kim attacks, first with a vertical attack aimed right at her enemies head, which was intended to be a fake out, and at the same time the true attack is a horizontal slash, separating his body at the waist. The warrior falls to the ground with a thud in two pieces dying. The first \of the two warriors catches up to Kim and she is ready to end this battle. She leaps from the trees to the ground and moves out of the way of enemy in time to have a chance to take his head off'; however, as she swings her blades, the warrior produces and short dagger that he uses to block the swords and removes his own from the sheath on his back. The battle continues in a series of slashes from each combatant, however, neither is getting the upper hand. On one of her blocked slashes Kim connects with a low round kick that takes her enemy down to one knee, and she presses her advantage with another flurry of sword slashes which is meant to disarm her opponent. As the sword slashes succeed in their intended purpose she brings the blade in her left hand back around and ends the battle by taking off her enemies head. Seeing that her battle is over she resheaths her blades and heads back to where Joseph is fighting his foes.

Joseph, quite different from the way Kim started her battle, starts his off in an offensive posture. He attacks his enemies first with just his hands and feet. He lands several punches to the midsection of one enemy, while connecting with several kicks to the midsection and head of the other. The two Black Shinobi Warriors retaliate in much the same way with several kicks and *punches, most of which Joseph manages to block or dodge in one way shape or form; however, a few attacks do get through his defenses. Towards the end of their attacks, one lands a punch to Joseph's stomach, which doubles him over, and sets him up for a high knee from the other that he takes in his face, and gets sent flying backwards and lands on his back. Not wanting to give his opponents anymore of an advantage then they already have, he quickly gets to his feet and goes back on the attack. He lands a hard blow to one of his enemies temples, which sends him staggering backwards, the other seeing this draws his weapon, a three sectional staff and attacks with it to give his comrade some time to recover from the blow. Joseph dodging the attacks made with the three sectional staff manages to draw one of his swords, and starts using it to block the attacks meant for his head. Even though he manages to block the majority of the strikes his is still hit by an overhead strike that manages to go over his blade. Dazed momentarily by this strike the enemy presses his advantage and continues his assault, now joined by his comrade. Joseph, dodging the attacks more by instinct than anything else, comes to his senses, and draws his other sword to be able to block and strike simultaneously. Blocking a strike from a blade, Joseph sees out of the corner of his eye an attack with the three sectional staff coming at him from his right side, aiming with the blade in his right hand he slashes through the chain link in the staff, removing one of the sections, causing that separated section to go flying off into the high grass far behind Joseph. Using the shock that he just caused, he quickly lashes out with a sidekick while at the same time knocks the sword he had blocked to the side knocking the other Black Shinobi Warrior off balance momentarily. Taking the opportunity to even the odds he quickly comes back across with the sword in his left hand and removes the head of the sword bearing warrior. Now being able to focus completely on the one enemy Joseph resumes his attack. Charging his enemy with a flurry of slashes from his swords, he manages to separate the already damaged weapon of his enemy into two separate parts, and before his enemy can recover, he uses the opening he just created and cuts his enemy into two pieces with a vertical sword slash with the sword in his right hand, much the same way as he did with the three sectional staff. Seeing that the fight is over and that Kim has arrived back to the location where the battle began, Joseph resheaths his blade and takes a long, deep, breath.*

Kim (breathing heavily)- I think that is all of them, where to now?

Joseph (starting to walk in the direction to the others)- Now we meet up with our comrades. Let's go, it's getting dark, and I don't want to be out here when the sun is down.

Joseph and Kim start on their journey to meet with Kenneth and Crystal. As they move through the forested area on the path, they find themselves talking to pass the time that the trip takes.

Joseph (looking back over his shoulder)- You said you could help us, how?

Kim (looking around nervously)- I've been to Ryan's temple many times. The reason for both being there and for his burning my village is the same, he wanted to take me for his wife, I refused on several occasions, his retribution was the burning of my village.

Joseph (with sympathy in his voice)- I see, no wonder you have so much anger in you, and now I understand the reason you want vengeance on him, you feel responsible for the death of your village (stopping aburtly). Kim that wasn't your fault, you can't blame yourself, although, I certainly understand why you do. From what you told me I take it you know the way to the Black Shinobi Temple, and what dangers we may face on our way there.

Kim (looking into his eyes)- Yes I do, and I will help you in any way I can.

Joseph (looking into her eyes)- That is all I can ask. We better get moving again, where I left the others isn't too far ahead.

By the time Joseph and Kim return to the spot where the others are, Kenneth and Crystal have finished setting up camp and have started cooking dinner for the group. As they eat Kim goes over the route that will take them to the Black Shinobi Temple.

Kim (looking at each of the others in turn but letting her gaze linger on Joseph for a few seconds longer before she starts)- Alright, this is the route I know. This path is the first part of the route, as far as I know we are in no danger on this path, unless, we're attacked by the Black Shinobi again. The first real danger will come in the next leg of the route, the valley of the volcano. In this valley there are areas where steam will just shoot out of nowhere, lava pits, of course an active volcano, for which the valley is named of, and finally, the greatest threat there, the creature of the valley. This creature is made of the strongest lava rocks, and is as tall as a two story building. It is immensely powerful too. If we can we want to avoid a fight with that creature, if we can't, let's hope we can defeat it as quickly as possible. The next leg of our journey takes us across a plateau. I personally haven't seen anything that could pose a danger to us, however, it is rumored that the fabled dog of the underworld, Cerberus, roams that area, if this is true, we may be in for some trouble if he finds us. After the plateau, we follow a path up a mountain, the path is safe, but, there are three creatures there, one made of stone, one made of earth, and one that can control the element of fire. After that we have to go by boat to an island in the center of a great lake which is guarded by a merman, then, we will be at the temple.

Kenneth (looking at Kim from the other side of the fire)- How many days will it take us to reach the temple?

Kim (turning to look at Kenneth)- Roughly three to five days, depending on how quick we can move, and if we run into any unexpected trouble.

Joseph (standing up and stretching)- Well then, we all best get some rest, our journey continues tomorrow.

The other three warriors take Joseph's suggestion to heart and as Kenneth, Crystal, and Joseph unroll their sleeping bags, Joseph notices that Kim hasn't moved from where she was sitting next to the fire.

Joseph (walking over to Kim)- You didn't really come prepared for this did you?

Kim (holding her arms across her chest and rubbing them to keep them warm)- I guess not.

Joseph (taking a deep breath and letting it out)- I barely know you, and you're already being a pain in my ass (chuckles) or I'm just too nice, for tonight you can use mine. Don't try to argue with me, you won't win, besides, I managed to find a blanket that I could use in case something happened to the sleeping bag. Tomorrow, on our journey to the valley of the volcano, we'll see if we can find you a sleeping bag.

Kim (wrapping her arms around Joseph)- Thank you.

The two move from the fire to where Joseph's bag is. As Kim gets into the sleeping bag Joseph digs into his bag and pulls out the blanket that he mentioned to Kim and moves back over to the fire for the added warmth and the two fall asleep after a few minutes.

CHAPTER FIVE

THE VALLEY OF
THE VOLCANO

The next morning finds the four warriors preparing for their day's journey. While Joseph, Kenneth, and Crystal are packing their bags and making sure that they have everything they need, Kim is cooking them breakfast on the still roaring fire from the night before. As the three finish packing their bags and taking the inventory of their gear they make their way over to the fire and are given a plate of food by Kim, however, she gives Joseph a little more than the food.

Kim (kissing Joseph on the cheek)- How did you sleep?

Joseph (eyes going wide in surprise)- I slept fine. What was the Kiss for?

Kim (going and sitting down next to him)- My way of saying thank you for letting me use your sleeping bag last night.

Joseph (regaining his composure)- Not a problem. Now how far away are we from the valley?

Kim (going completely serious in mannerisms and voice tone)- We should be there at noon, and then it will take us the rest of the day to cross it. The most dangerous area to cross will be towards the end, cause that is where the active volcano is as well as the creature.

Joseph (bring his right hand up onto his forehead as if he has to hold his head to keep it from falling)- I see, what is the best way to avoid any trouble in this area?

Kim (looking them all in the eyes one after another before she answers)- Move fast and stay as quiet as we can.

As the four finish eating, Joseph, Kenneth, and Crystal grab their bags and follow Kim on the trail to the valley of the volcano. Little do they know that their presence and conversation has not gone unnoticed.

Hooded figure 2 (rubbing his hands together)- Now this one will have a chance to avenge this one's fallen comrade. To the valley of the volcano they go, but come out, never shall they.

As the four continue on their journey, they stop at the ruins of an old city, and manage to find enough food and water to replenish their supplies as well as a pack and sleeping bag for Kim. After replenishing their packs, the leave the city and shortly after noon, they come to the valley of the volcano.

Kim (turning to face the others)- This is the start of the valley. When we go in here you have to be extremely alert to avoid getting blasted by scolding hot pockets of steam, as well as avoiding weak areas of the ground where molten lava could still be underneath.

Crystal (looking at Joseph and Kenneth)- Well if you boys need any help us ladies will be right here. Hahahah. Lets go.

As the four enter the valley Joseph and Kim take the point position, with Crystal following behind them and finally, Kenneth in the rear guard position. Thirty minutes pass and already they have had several near encounters with steam pockets, as well as having the ground give out beneath them to discover that there is a pit of molten lava under foot. Shortly after the last discovery of a lava pit, Crystal is forced to jump to the right to avoid being blasted by a steam pocket and as she lands on the ground, the ground gives way to drop her into a molten lava pit. Kenneth being the closest to her leaps down to catch her and as he does so hits the wall on the far side of the lava pit to propel himself upwards and out of danger. He lands to the right side of the pit and puts Crystal down.

Kenneth (panting from the near death experience and to catch his breath)- I….thought….. you said….. it would be me and Joseph that would need the help.

Crystal (blushing from embarrassment)- Guess I was wrong.

As the four share a laugh from this exchange, they also realize just how dangerous this valley is and how important it is to get out of it as quickly as possible. As they realize this they continue their journey to get to the end of the valley, and hope that they come across no other dangers. As the day comes to a close they manage to get to the end of the valley without any other near disasters.

Crystal (seeing the end of the valley and projecting relief in her voice)- There it is the end of the valley, we made it.

Kenneth (unconsciously raising his voice.)- WE REALLY MADE IT!!!!!!!!!!!!!

Joseph (turning to Kenneth quickly)- Kenneth, quiet. We're not out of this yet, remember, the creature.

Kenneth (bring his right hand up to cover his eyes) Oh man, I can't believe how stupid I just was. I hope it didn't hear me.

As the four start to move again, Joseph hears loud noises coming their way and he turns to see, hoping, but, already knowing deep down in his gut what is coming after them. As Joseph turns to see the creature running up behind them, he notices that it is getting ready to throw a giant ball of semi-solid lava directly at them.

**Joseph (shouting at the top of his lungs while running)-
EVERYONE SCATTER!!!!!!!!!!!!!!**

*Just as he yells this to his comrades the creature throws the lava
ball. Everyone but Kim was able to react quick enough to avoid
being hit by the lava ball, Joseph, seeing this, makes a desperate
leap to grab Kim, hoping that the momentum he had from running
would be enough to carry both Kim and himself out of harm's way.
Joseph's leap of hope pays of; but, just barely, because he manages
to move Kim and himself, through his built up momentum, out of
the way of the lava ball just as it passes them. The two quickly get
to their feet, and move even quicker to take cover.*

Joseph (yelling to everyone)- Is everyone okay?

**Kim, Kenneth, Crystal (in unison)- Yeah. What should
we do?**

**Joseph (pausing for a moment, then taking a stance
to summon his armor)- Everyone, summon your armor.
(without waiting for a reply) ARMOR OF SHINOBI,
IGNITE!!!!!!!!!!!!!!!!!!!!!!!!**

*Just as Joseph did, the three others summon their armor, and
in doing so are engulfed in white flames. As the flames die down,
the warriors leap from the cover of the rocks and start attacking the
creature. Kim, putting on a burst of speed, draws her swords and
leaps two stories into the air to attack the creature with a spinning
slash to the head. Unfortunately she doesn't even get close enough
to land the blow because the creature swats her away like she is
just an annoying little fly with a hand that is the size of a small
boulder. Kim, from the impact of the creatures attack, goes soaring
through the air to strike a lava rock wall with enough force to leave
an imprint of her armored body in the face of the wall, the fall
to the ground, twisting in mid-air to hit the ground on her back.
Seeing what happened to Kim in her attempt at a frontal assault,
Kenneth decides on a different tactic. Running directly towards the
creature, using all the power he can muster in his legs, he leaps over*

the creature, performing a twisting flip that will bring him down behind the creature and facing it. Upon hitting the ground, he uses his momentum to left him into the air and pulls his three sectional staff off of his back and strikes at the back of the creature's neck. The creature feeling the impact of the weapon, turns with more speed then thought possible, on Kenneth and with a smile on it's face, even before Kenneth lands on the ground, kicks Kenneth high into the air, and then as he comes down to the creatures shoulders, the creature hits Kenneth with a punch that sends him sailing twenty feet through the air before hitting the ground, and causes him to bounce another five feet upon hitting the ground. While surveying the carnage that it has caused to Kenneth, the creature gets surprised to feel something strike it in its back with enough force to move it a couple of feet. Turning again with amazing speed the creature sees Crystal standing roughly fifty feet away from it with her bow draw, shooting arrows at it. In a rage at being injured by her and her weapon it charges her. Seeing the creature's distraction with Crystal, Joseph, dashes at the creature and when he is five feet in front of the creature leaps into the air and lands an upper cut, with his armored fist, that, to everyone's surprise, sends the creature to the ground. The creature, recovering from it's shock of being knocked to the ground, quickly looks for something it can throw, and sees a small boulder. As Joseph moves in to press the attack, the creature, simultaneously, grabs the boulder and with its right foot knocks Joseph to the ground. Getting to its feet, the creature quickly takes aim and hurls the boulder and Crystal, who unsuccessfully attempts to dodge it. The boulder not only hits her, but, carries her with it to smash into the same wall that Kim was knocked into. As she impacts against the wall and the boulder against her, the boulder falls to the ground, and she falls from where she impacted against the wall to hit the boulder and bounce to the ground. Joseph, getting to his feet, sees that he is the only one left to fight this creature, and knowing that not only his life is on the line but the lives of his comrades and friends are on the line as well, finally draws his twin katanas. Leaping into action, Joseph throws several attacks with both his feet and his blades. He attacks the creature with his blades at the knees with leaping vertical and horizontal strikes that seem to have no effect on the creature. In retaliation the creature throws a downward punch at Joseph, which he jumps out of the way of. The creatures fist smashes into the ground. Joseph seeing a great chance, leaps onto the creatures arm, and using a speed even he didn't know he had, runs up the creatures arm to land a vivacious flying sidekick to the creatures head, which sends the creature reeling to the side. Joseph follows up this attack with a combination of sword slashes to the creatures head that actually do damage. The creature instinctively bats at the shoulder Joseph is on, knocking him off and to land hard on his back on the ground. The creature in a rage, attempts to literally stomp Joseph out of existence. Joseph, recovering just in time to see this, rolls out of the way of the creature's incoming foot. Quickly regaining his footing, Joseph leaps backwards to put some distance between the creature and himself.

Joseph (combining his swords)- I think it's time we ended this.

The creature seeing that Joseph isn't moving from where he landed charges Joseph.

Joseph (leaps three stories into the air at the charging creature)- ARMOR OF SHINOBI, FLARE UP NOW!!!!!! !!!

After Joseph calls out this command, his armor and swords start to admit a blinding, white light, and as he descends through the air he slashes the creature in half vertically and then again horizontally, creating a glowing cross going from top to bottom, and side to side of the create. When Joseph lands on the ground he spins and disconnects his swords while his back is to the creature and as he resheathes his swords, the creature can be seen exploding behind him. As the creature explodes, Joseph falls to one knee in exhaustion.

As he tries to catch his breath he hears a loud noise, almost like the sound of a plane crashing, to his right. As he hears this noise he snaps his head to the right.

Joseph (in annoyance) – SHIT!!!!!!!!! I can't believe this.

As Joseph sees that the volcano to his right is erupting, he looks around and finds the Kenneth lying 25 yards in front of him while Kim and Crystal are 25 yards behind him. Luckily Kim is coming around.

Joseph (yelling in an urgent tone)- KIM, Crystal up, and if you can't wake her, carry her out of here.

After having said this to Kim, Joseph dashes over to where Kenneth is and starts trying to bring him around, while Kim is doing the same to Crystal. As Kim gets to Crystal, she starts to shake her violently and seeing that didn't work, tries slapping her in the face. As she slaps Crystal, Crystal starts to wake up, and is quite angry about being slapped in the first place.

Crystal (raising it to a sitting position looking as though she is about to punch Kim dead in the face)- What the hell??!!!!!!!!!!!!!!!

Kim (with an apologetic tone and a shrug of her shoulders)- Sorry it was the only way I could wake you. (pointing at the volcano) We gotta get out of here, otherwise we're dead.

Crystal following to where Kim's finger is pointing to see that the volcano is erupting gets to her feet as quickly as if she had never be knocked out, and the two of them start to head for the end of the valley. Meanwhile, Joseph has gotten to where Kenneth is lying and is attempting to wake him through violently shaking him, and just as Kim woke Crystal, slapping him across the face; however, he is having no luck in waking him. Looking in the direction of the erupting volcano, he decides he has no more time to waste, and hoisting the unconscious Kenneth onto his shoulders he starts a dead sprint to get both him and his friend out of the soon to be lava filled battle area of the valley. As he catches up with Kim and Crystal, they all look and decide the best way to get out of danger is to keep running until they are out of the valley and onto the plateau. They run as fast as they can, and fifteen minutes later, they arrive at the plateau. Seeing that Kenneth is still unconscious, the other three decide to keep going forward for another half hour, and then make camp until the morning.

CHAPTER SIX

THE PLATEAU

As the four warriors rest for the rest of the night, Kim, Crystal, and Joseph take turns keeping an eye on the unconscious form of Kenneth. As the darkness gives way to light, Kim and Crystal awaken to find Joseph sitting near his friend, keeping an eye on him. As the two female warriors head towards Joseph to reassure him, Kenneth starts to stir.

Kenneth (rubbing his head as he wakes)- Did anyone get the number of that train that hit me.

Joseph (showing his relief by relaxing)- Don't worry about that train, as you call it, it isn't going to do any of us anymore harm.

Kenneth (trying to get up)- I'm guessing we're on the plateau.

Joseph (helping Kenneth to his feet)- Yeah, you were out the entire night, let's get some food in you and then we can start across this place.

As Joseph helps Kenneth over to the fire that has been burning all night and is now being used by Kim to cook their breakfast, Crystal comes over to help support Kenneth's weight. As the three get to their places around the fire, Kim sets a plate of food in front of everyone, and it is very clear just how relieved everyone is that

Kenneth is alright. After the four warriors finish their breakfast, they grab their already packed bags and start their journey across the plateau. Little do they know that in the shadows, a familiar figure is lurking, waiting for the right time to strike. After several hours, the four come upon a field where there are many plants, and among the plants are some flowers. The beauty of the flowers catches all of them off guard.

Crystal (wide-eyed amazement)- I can't believe that something so beautiful is in the path to the most evil place ever known.

Joseph (understanding at the site)- Even places where evil is near have area of beauty, I guess you could say it's a way that the light tries to battle back the darkness. Let's go ahead and rest here for a while.

The four warriors lay their packs on the ground and pull some water and food out to eat. As the eat they admire the beauty of the area they are in; however, they aren't resting alone, for unknown to them a dark figure hides in the shadows, observing them and plotting to exact his revenge for the death of his comrade. During the warriors break from the traveling, some of them sleep after eating, and some just admire the scenery; but, even during their break at least one always remains alert, ready to warn the others if danger should come their way.

Kim (walking up beside Joseph)- Mind if I sit with you?

Joseph (looking up at her)- Not at all. (hearing Kenneth snoring in the background and chuckling to himself about it) I can't believe he is sleeping, you would think he got enough rest last night after being knocked out by that creature.

Kim (laughing)- I know right. I think we should get moving again, this plateau is pretty large, and it will take some time to cross, at least two days.

Joseph (nodding in agreement)- Your right, and it's getting late in the day, we should start moving again. You go wake Crystal, I'll take sir snore-a-lot over there.

Joseph and Kim go to wake the other two and shortly after that they start moving again. After another four hours of travel they come across an area that is shaded by trees. Deciding that it is getting to late to continue, they set up camp and get a fire ready to cook dinner and to keep themselves warm; however, a shadow in the darkness of the trees prepares himself to strike at his comrade's killer. As the four warriors ready themselves for bed, the dark figure, sensing the time is right, starts his attack. He leaps out of the shadows and rushes towards Kenneth. As he nears his prey, he draws a sword, and Kenneth sensing the danger, moves to the side just in time to avoid having his head removed from his shoulders. The other three turn to see what is going on, but, just as quickly as the shadow appeared it vanishes, and all that is left is a voice talking in the darkness.

Hooded figure 2- I have come to avenge my comrade. You who avoided my attack, I challenge you to a life or death duel.

Kenneth (looking around to try and spot the owner of the voice)- Very well, I accept your challenge; however, you'll regret it.

The dark figure appears again, sword in hand, ready to fight Kenneth. Without a moment's hesitation, the dark figure charges Kenneth. As the figure draws near, he slashes with his sword at Kenneth's head, which Kenneth ducks under. As the dark figure continues his spin, he draws a knife in a reverse grip and attempts to stab Kenneth in his side. Kenneth, seeing the strike coming blocks the attack with his left hand by snaking it up under the figures left hand and making contact with the figures wrist, while counterattacking with a thrust punch to his enemy's stomach. The power behind Kenneth's strike moves his enemy backwards a few feet. With the newly created distance between them, Kenneth starts to talk.

Kenneth (walking a little to his right as he talks)- I have to admit, you seem to be a better fighter than your comrade was, I guess that means I should get properly ready. (taking a stance to call his armor) ARMOR OF SHINOBI, IGNITE!!!!!!!!!!!!!!!!!!!!!!!!!!!!

Even before the white flames die down, Kenneth leaps through them, weapon in hand charging his opponent. As he nears he hurls the three sectional staff to it full length at him, hoping to catch him off guard. The dark figure, surprised to see his enemy leaping through the flames, barely notices the weapon extending towards him. Luckily with the knife in his left hand he manages to deflect the attack at the last second causing Kenneth to yank the staff back to him. With the staff flying through the air back to Kenneth's hand, the dark figure races towards him, preparing to attack with an overhand slash with his sword. Kenneth's full staff returns to him just in time for him to block the overhand attack with the center area, and counter with an attack to his enemy's right temple with the left part of his staff. The dark figure manages to avoid the blow, by using one of his abilities, literally fading into the shadows. Kenneth, caught off guard by his opponents ability leaps back, and puts himself into a guard position. Then all of a sudden he hear the menacing voice of his opponent coming from every direction.

Hooded figure 2- HAHAHAHAH!!!!!!!! I should have warned you, I am a shadow hunter, and my power is at it's peak at night. You haven't a chance in hell, with the land soaked in darkness, I can strike from anywhere, at anytime.

As dark figure finishes speaking, he leaps out of a shadow behind Kenneth and strikes him in the back with a flying side kick that sends him to the ground face first. Kenneth gets to his feet in time to see his enemy melt away into the shadows again without a trace only to appear again on his right side to land a vivacious punch to the side of his face that spins him around. Kenneth, hoping to use the momentum of the spin to his advantage, tries to strike with his left hand, but, to his dismay, his fist goes right through the area where his opponent should have been. Getting his bearings, Kenneth see's that his enemy has vanished into the darkness once again. Looking around in a vain attempt to spot his enemy, he gets blindsided by a roundhouse kick to his ribs that doubles him over, then instead of seeing, he feels the dark figures knee connect with his head. The force of the attack causes his upper body to fly backwards to cause him to topple over onto his back. As he hits the ground, he uses the momentum to somersault backwards onto his feet. Seeing his enemy coming towards him, he swings his staff and just before it connects with his enemy he vanishes, and just as quickly reappears in front of him to catch him with a stiff uppercut under the chin sending him up into the air a couple of feet, and before he even hits the ground the dark figure runs up beside and grabs him in midair and throws him another three feet. The dark figure presses his advantage and goes to end the battle with a killing strike from his sword; however, Kenneth, playing possem sees the attack coming and traps the dark figures sword with his three sectional staff while at the same time sweeping his legs out from under him. As the figure hits the ground, he disappears into the darkness of the shadows, and Kenneth quickly gets to his feet.

Kenneth (gripping his weapon)- I see the only way I'll win this is by taking away your advantage of being able to hide in the shadows.

Hooded figure 2- To bad for you, there is no way for you to do that.

Kenneth (starting to smile)- I might have a way to do that.

Hooded figure 2- Oh really, what would that be?

Kenneth (sliding his hands to the outside portions of his three sectional staff)- This: SOLAR FLARE TRIPLE STR IKE!!!!!!!!!!!!!!!!!!!!!!!!!!!!!!!!!!!

As Kenneth calls forth this ability, his armor starts to glow as bright as the sun, and his three sectional staff becomes an extention of that power, as if he were truly the sun and his staff a solar flare. As the power grows stronger, it starts to illuminate the entire area, and he sees his enemy and charge. The dark figure, blinded by the light being given off, doesn't see Kenneth charging him, and thus, doesn't see the end of the three sectional staff coming towards his midsection, the impact doubles him over, as Kenneth snaps the end of the staff into his hand to enfold with the center portion, he drives the center of the staff into the face of his enemy, sending him several feet into the air, and finally leaping into the air while at the same time twisting the staff in his hand so that the only piece he hasn't attacked with was in a position to attack he starts twirling it over his head, with his leap carrying him far above his enemy, he thrust the final portion of the staff at him, and as it connects his enemy is engulfed in sun like flames that incinerate him on contact. As he walks back to the others his armor starts to fade from his body, and the darkness starts to return to the area.

Joseph (walking up to his friend)- Are you alright?

Kenneth (putting a hand on Joseph's shoulder)- Yeah, I'm fine, I just need to get a little sleep now.

Crystal (fists on her hips)- Why did you fight on your own? You didn't have to.

Kenneth (looking at her)- I know, I guess you could say I was a matter of honor, he challenged me and me alone, it wouldn't have been fair if we all fought him. (heading to his sleeping bag)Let's get some sleep now, we still have a long journey ahead of us.

Joseph (walking up behind Kenneth and looking directly at Crystal)- I agree with Kenneth, we still do have a long journey ahead of us, and we do need our rest.

The four warriors head to where their respective sleeping bags are next to the fire. As the other three climb into them Joseph sits on his starting their rotation of guard for the night. Later that night, Crystal takes his place, then Kim, and finally Kenneth. As daylight draws near, Kenneth makes sure the other three are up and moving as he packs his bag. After packing their bags they start their journey again. As the group walks along the path that they have chosen, some admire the scenery of different plants, and continue to wonder how things of such beauty can exist in such an evil place, still the others decide to keep their senses alert for any possible trouble. As mid-day comes, the group stops to rest and eat.

Joseph (looking around as he eats)- Well so far nothing has happened today. Listen, I know we all like the scenery, but, keep your guard up, who knows when, or who will attack us.

Kenneth (putting his drink down)- We know, don't worry, when and if we are attacked we'll handle it.

Joseph (nodding at Kenneth)- Alright, lets finish eating and get on our way.

As the four finish their respective meals, they sling their bags onto their backs and head out to continue their mission. As the time goes by, they find themselves out of the area where all the beauty was and find themselves in a part of the plateau that is littered with the bones of many different species, dogs, deer, birds, and even humans. As the four warriors examine the area they are in, Kim, hearing something large coming up behind them turns to see the three headed hound, Cerberus.

Kim (yelling to the others)- We gotta get out of here.

As the warriors scatter, Cerberus, from his center head launches a gigantic fireball right at Joseph. Kim seeing that he won't be able to avoid it, decides to repay the favor. Running to his aid, she gets within a legs length of him, seeing how close the fireball is she takes a chance and catches the fireball with a furious roundhouse kick that sends it right back at Cerberus; however, the beast manages to protect himself from the sudden attack, using a blast of ice from its left head.

Joseph (taking Kim with him to a shielded area)- Are you alright?

Kim (with concern in her voice) Forget me, are you okay?

Joseph (smile on his face and relief in his voice)- Yeah, I'm fine, and judging by the way you're acting I would say you're okay too. (to the others)Alright, lets teach this dog who it's master is, call your armor! (taking his stance)ARMOR OF SHINOBI, IGNITE!!!!!!!!!!!!!!!!!!!!!!!!!!!

As the four warriors are engulfed in flames, Cerberus charges at them. As the beast nears them, leaping through the flames, wearing his armor, Joseph charges the beast, and as he nears Cerberus, he leaps into the air, and knocks the dog to the ground with an uppercut under its middle head.

Joseph (takes up his fighting stance)- Bad dog, time for you to be taught a lesson.

As Cerberus gets back to his feet and shakes the cobwebs from all three of his heads, Kenneth, Crystal, and Kim come up beside Joseph. Cerberus's right head lets out a vicious howl and looks down at the warriors with a glare that shows nothing more than a bloodlust. Then with no warning at all, from the right head, lightning bolts shot from his mouth, causing the warriors to leap in all directions to avoid being hit. As Kim get to her feet, she sees that she is the closest to the beast, she draws her swords and leaps up onto the center head of the beast, this action causes the other two heads to start attacking her, as she dodges their biting attacks she slashes at their heads with the swords and attempts to stab one of her swords into the center head of the beast. As the left and right head of the beast try to grab her in their fangs, one of them knocks her to the ground with it's snout. She hits the ground with a loud thud, and the left head of the beast attacks her with it's ice blast. By this time Joseph is nearby, seeing the danger she is in, he races towards the left head of the beast, leaps into the air and nails the side of the left head with a flying side kick causing the blast of ice to miss wide to Kim's right. Using the distraction that Joseph caused Crystal while at a distance lets an arrow fly at the right head of the beast. The arrow grazes the right head by it's right ear. Kenneth also seizing the opportunity, extends his three sectional staff to its full length striking under the jaw of the beast's center head, causing that head to fly backwards, and causing a howl of pain to escape from all three heads at the same time. Kim, using the opportunity provided by Joseph, gets to her feet and heads to where Joseph has landed on the ground after delivering that divesting attack on the beast. By the time she reaches him, Cerberus has recovered from his pain, and swipes at them with it's left paw, attempting to slice them into bloody ribbons with his claws. Joseph seeing the beast's attack, quickly turns while drawing his swords and blocks the attack, however, the beast unbelievable strength starts to push Joseph back. Kim, seeing that Joseph is being overpowered by the beast, rushes in and slashes at the leg of the beast, causing it to recoil in pain, and allowing Joseph and Kim enough time to escape his reflexive counter attack. As Joseph and Kim retreat out of range of the beast's claws, Kenneth is fending off attacks from the right head of the beast, while at the same time delivering counter attacks with not only his staff; but, his feet as well. Kenneth eventually nails the beast's right head with his staff that it actually sends that head reeling to the side, allowing Kenneth enough time to escape to a safe range as well. As Kenneth rejoins the others they decide on a different course of attack. Kenneth and Crystal head to the flanks of the beast. Once there, Joseph and Kim charge up the middle, when the near the beast, Kim leaps over him to land behind it, then rebounds to come down on it back, with her swords stabbing right into the center of the beasts back, Joseph meanwhile continues his charge till he gets under the beast, and once there, he slashes at the belly of the beast. Kenneth and Crystal, seeing that the beast is distracted by the pain being caused by their comrades, attack the heads of the beast with multiple blows from Kenneth's staff, and the edges of Crystal's bow, causing the creature to spill it's blood on the ground. The creature coming to it's senses, leaps forward into the air to get away from it's attackers on the ground and while in the air it's left head reaches back and knocks Kim off of it with his snout. Kim hitting the ground hard, starts to get to her feet as the others are running to her. As the others join her, the beast looks at them with nothing but a blood rage in it's eyes.

Joseph (looking at the beast)- We have to end this now.

Crystal (looking over at Joseph)- Yeah, but how?

Joseph (looking at both Crystal and Kim)- You two, use the greatest of your powers on that beast. Kenneth, you and I will serve as a distraction.

Kenneth (looking at Joseph)- Alright. Let's teach this dog one of our tricks.

Kim and Crystal leap backwards, preparing themselves to attack Cerberus with the greatest abilities. As the two girls leap back, Joseph and Kenneth Charge the beast head on, and as the charge him, the girls ready their weapon. Crystal draws an arrow and sets it in place on her bow, while Kim combines her swords at the hilt, with the blades reversed so the edges are facing away from each other.

Crystal- SHOOTING STAR ARROW!!!!!!!!!!!!!!!!!!!!!!!!!

Kim- SPINNING BLADES OF FLAME!!!!!!!!!!!!!!!!!!!!!

Crystal letting the arrow fly from her bow, the arrow gains all the strength and spend of a shooting star, while Kim throws her combined swords at the beast, and as they spin, the blade literally become engulfed in flames as well as the source of them. Crystal's arrow hits the right head of the beast incinerating that head, while Kim's swords strike the left head slashing through the neck like a hot knife through butter. Seeing that the beast is not yet dead, but, that it has gone completely insane now, Joseph and Kenneth fall back to where Kim and Crystal are. As they get there Kim's swords return to her hand and she seperates them.

Joseph (looking at the beast in aw and pity)- I have to admit, I'm impressed by the beast's strength. But it is time to put him out of his misery.

Joseph starts to walk towards the beast, looking into the beasts insane eyes. The beast charges Joseph. As the beast charges Joseph, it starts to gather energy into it mouth creating a massive fire ball; however, Joseph stops in his tracks and takes a stance with his right leg half a foot length behind his left and legs spread shoulder width apart, he chambers his hands on his right side, and gathers a pure white energy in them, as the beast spits its massive fireball from its mouth, Joseph, keeping his hands together at the wrist, thrusts his hands forward while twisting them, and leaning on his front leg and completely extending his back leg, shoots a massive stream of white energy at the beast, that goes through the fireball, causing it to collapse on itself, and strikes the beast, incinerating it on contact. As Joseph recovers from his attack, the other three warriors join him.

Kenneth (placing a hand on Joseph's armored shoulder)- Nice, I didn't think you would be able to do that attack this soon.

Joseph (turning his head to look at Kenneth)- What was that attack?

Kenneth (removing his hand from Joseph's shoulder)- It is called the Shinobi Blast, and only the strongest of the Shinobi Masters have been able to use it.

Joseph (takes a deep breath and releases it)- How many other abilities will I find I have? We better get moving.

As the four leave the battle area, the armor they were wearing leaves their bodies. The warriors travel for another two hours before they reach the end of the plateau, and see the beginning of the mountain they must pass over.

CHAPTER SEVEN

THE MOUNTAIN

As the five warriors arrive at the base of the mountain, they see a path leading up it, and start their trek to the top.

Joseph (looks over to Kim)- So how long will it take us to reach the top of the mountain?

Kim (looking back at Joseph)- We should be able to reach the top before night fall; but, it's not reaching the top that concerns me, it's what we will find at the top.

Kenneth (looking back at Kim)- What do you mean?

Kim (stopping where she is)- You all remember the creatures I told you about that await us at the top of this mountain, the only way the group of Black Shinobi where able to get by them was to appease them, or to have Ryan with them. It's rumored that anyone who tried to fight these creatures was defeated and killed. I don't know how or the powers that all of them have; but, I've heard stories about weaknesses.

Crystal (turning to face Kim)- Well tell us, what are the stories you've heard?

Kim (getting a faraway look in her eyes)- First off, if there is more than one person challenging them, they will only allow one person at a time to fight. I haven't heard of anyone that has managed to fight them and live past the first battle. There is a creature that is made of the earth. It is said that as long as his feet are on the ground, he has an endless supply of strength and can regenerate any part of his body that has been removed or injured, so it would seem the way to beat him would be to get him off the ground and keep him off of it. Next there is one made of stone. I've never heard of this one being injured in any way. So I can't speculate on any weakness he has. The last one is a creature that can control fire. They say this one is the oldest among the trio, and has only one weakness, his own flames. To beat him we have to somehow turn his own flames against him. Everything I know about these three, you now know, keep in mind though that it is just hearsay.

Joseph (placing his hands on Kim's shoulders)- It's alright, you know what they say, in every story there is a little truth to it, so we just have to hope that the parts in your story of their weaknesses is true, if not, we'll still find a way to beat them.

Kim (shakes her head and her eyes start to water)- It's not good enough, hoping that what I told you is true, these creatures have never been beaten.

Kenneth (with a grin on his face)- There is a first time for everything. Come on let's get moving again

The four turn and start moving up the mountain again, as they move Kim clears the water from her eyes that was threatening to become tears. As they continue their journey, they don't make it too far from their last position, because as they are moving up the mountain four throwing spikes, one in front of each warrior, find their way into the ground at an angle, and as they look in the direction that they came from they see four figures clad in light weight, black armor.

Kenneth (stepping forward and examining the four figures with his fists posted on his hips)- Well this is new to me. I haven't ever come across a Black Shinobi that looks like them.

Joseph (coming to stand beside Kenneth, his hands contracted into fists)- So what do you think?

Kenneth (placing his right hand on his chin in a thinking posture)- If I had to guess, I'd say the assassin ranks of the Black Shinobi got an upgrade.

Joseph- My thoughts exactly. What do you think, use our armor?

Kenneth (letting his right hand drop to his side)- Yeah, in this case we don't know what they are capable of, so I would be a little more cautious than usual.

Joseph (a grin on his face)- I had a feeling. Alright guys, you heard the man, let's do it.

The four take identical positions, their feet spread shoulder with apart and their arms crossed at their chest. After assuming this position, at the same time they call out ARMOR OF SHINOBI, IGNITE, and all four are engulfed in flames. As the flames die down the four emerge, weapons in hand, ready for the battle.

Joseph (looking at one of the black figures that is wearing a helmet)- The one with the helmet is mine. You guys got the rest.

Before anyone can say anything else the four armored assassins leap at their opponents drawing and attacking with their weapons. One draws sais, another a metal staff, a third uses nunchucks, and the final one, the one wearing the helmet draws two swords. As the one armed with sais leaps down at Kim, she blocks his attack with her swords, and seconds later after the assassin lands on his feet the two carry their battle into the forested area of the mountain, moving not only on the ground; but, through the trees as well. As they move through this forest they leap at each other and attack with slashes of their respective weapons, which the other either blocks or dodges at the last second until they get to a little clearing in the forest, and decide to finish the battle there. As the two enter the clearing the assassin leaps at Kim, attempting to take her head off her shoulders, however, Kim dodges the attack by leaping forward in the direction she was originally going and as she lands she brings the sword in her left hand around in a slash meant to remove the assassin's head. The assassin blocks the attack and then connects with a round kick to the back of Kim's armored head, which sends her to the ground, but, using the momentum caused be the fall, she goes into a shoulder roll and comes up on her feet, and turns just in time to spin out of the way of a stabbing attack and as she completes her spin, she slashes at the back of the armored assassin. The assassin feeling the blade against the armor of his back, goes into a shoulder roll of his own, and comes up out of range of her sword attacks. The two warriors stand looking at each other for a few moments, then charge each other. Kim as she nears the assassin, leaps into the air and connects first with a front kick to the sternum, and then a roundhouse kick to the temple of the assassin sending him to the ground. She follows up on her advantage as she lands on her feet with a downward slash at the assassin laying on the ground. The assassin seeing the attack coming, brings his sais up in the form of an "x" to block the attack, and as he blocks it, he manages to kick Kim's feet out from under her, sending her to the ground. As the two get to their feet, the assassin manages to get up before Kim, and attacks with a slash at her midsection from left to right. Kim, using the sword in her left hand, blocks the attack, while, with the other sword, attacks with a downward slash of her own, that the assassin manages to block with his other sai. The two, locked in this stance, trying to overpower each other discover that they are of equal strength and push away from one another. After pushing away from each other, the two warriors, standing in a defensive posture with weapons raised, again start sizing up each other. The two charge each other once again; however, *it is Kim that strikes first this time with an over head slash, which the assassin blocks, but Kim, bringing her right foot up, doubles the assassin over with a thrust kick to his stomach, then leaping into the air, connects with her left knee to his face, sending the assassin to the ground laying on his back in a daze. Before Kim hits the ground she reverses the grip she has on her swords and as she lands she impales the assassin with both of her swords, ending the battle. As the case with every other assassin in the Black Shinobi clan, this one vanishes into thin air slowly.*

As Kenneth's opponent comes flying at him, he brings his three-sectional staff into a defensive position and as his enemy connects, the impact drives him into the forest. Finally, the momentum comes to a halt as Kenneth impacts against an old tree, leaving an indentation of his body in it.

Kenneth (shoving the assassin back several steps)- So, it appears this is going to be a battle of the staffs. Your normal staff against my three-sectional staff, let's see who's is better.

Kenneth doesn't even give his opponent the chance to respond, he immediately charges the assassin. As he draws near he launches his staff with a thrust to it's full length in an attempt to get a devasting first strike in on his opponent, to the chest area. The assassin manages to dodge the attack, and get in close enough swinging his staff to strike Kenneth in his chest driving him backwards about two feet. Yanking his staff back into his hands and holding both of the end sections at the ends closest to him, he takes up his fighting stance and waits for his opponent to attack, which he doesn't have to wait for too long. The assassin charges, thrusting his staff straight forward at Kenneth's stomach. Kenneth, seeing the attack coming blocks it with one of the outer sections of his staff, knocking the attack to the side, then quickly stepping forward with his back leg, he strikes with the other end of the staff to the head of the assassin, causing him to stumble to the side. Kenneth, seeing the opportunity, follows up with a strike from the other end of the staff to the assassin's ribs. The assassin leaps back after the fury of Kenneth's last attack. Kenneth, sensing that he had done some serious damage to his opponent, charges him. Leaping into the air as he nears the assassin and while in the air, he folds all three parts of his staff together, and with a downward thrust punch, enhanced by the solidness of the staff in his hands, strikes at the top of his opponents head, driving him into the ground. After Kenneth lands the devastating attack on the assassin, he leaps backwards, and as he lands, he again, unfolds his staff into it's three sections, getting into his fighting stance. The assassin, slowly and unsteadly, gets to his feet. As he regains his balance, he brings his staff out in front of him, holding it vertically with both of his hands, then, he vanishes into the ground. Kenneth, caught by surprise by his opponents move, drops his guard momentarily, and pays for it, as the assassin comes bursting out of the ground and nails Kenneth under the jaw with his staff, and then flying through the air and disappears into a nearby tree. Then as suddenly as he disappeared into the tree, he reappears from one on Kenneth's side. Kenneth, barely seeing the assassin coming at him from out of the corner of his eye, manages to block the first attack by the assassin, but, the assassin manages to swing the back end of his staff at the side of Kenneth's head knocking him to the ground. Then using the momentum built up from the impact the assassin again puts distance between himself and Kenneth before vanishing into the ground. Kenneth, regaining his footing after being knocked to the ground, realizes that he can't rely on his eyes to stop his enemy anymore. Taking his fighting stance again, Kenneth closes his eyes and starts to concentrate on his environment. As if guided by an unknown force, Kenneth, brings his back foot forward while pivoting on his front foot to bring himself one hundred eighty degrees from the direction he facing and blocks an attack from his enemy with his staff. Opening his eyes and thrusting his back foot forward at the same time he catches the assassin in the stomach with a vicious thrust kick, knocking the wind out of him and doubling him over at the same time. *Pressing his advantage, Kenneth leaps into the air driving his knee into the assassin's face, breaking the nose, and sending the assassin flying backwards. As Kenneth comes flying down, he folds all three sections of his staff together in his right hand, then with a twist of his wrist, a spike comes out of the end of one of the sections of his staff. Crashing down onto the assassin, Kenneth drives the spike into the head of his enemy ending the battle, causing the assassin to disappear into nothingness.*

As the assassin with the nun-chucks comes flying through the air at Crystal, he changes his direction slightly while in midair which causes him to land on the ground right in front of her. Taking advantage of her momentary shock, he strikes her in her abdomen with his nun-chuck enhanced fists sending her into the air and into the trees at an angle and then follows. Crystal, landing hard on her back, realizes that her opponent sent her flying a good 20meters into the forest, and into a relatively small clearing. Before she can notice anything else about the area she is in, the assassin comes flying through the trees at her intending to drive his foot through her chest. Crystal, seeing what is about to happen, quickly rolls out of the way of the attack and manages to push herself quickly to her feet and brings her bow up in front of her in a defensive posture. The assassin knowing that his best chance of winning the battle lies at close range combat, closes the distance with Crystal and attacks with his nun-chucks.

Assassin (while attacking)- Your bow is a great weapon for long distance attacks, but, at close range, it's not worth shit. This is your last battle.

Crystal (fending off the assassin's attacks with a smile)- You underestimate my bow, how about I give you a closer look.

As Crystal blocks one of the assassin's horizontal attacks with his nun-chucks, she counter attacks with her bow, slicing not only into his armor, but, the skin underneath.

Assassin (covering his wound, and speaking in a surprised voice)- How did you do that, I don't understand.

Crystals (grinning holding her bow up showing the assassin his own blood on her bow)- Take a close look at this bow, and you'll notice it has an edge to it. The White Shinobi Clan learned long ago flaws of having their bowmen only skilled in long range combat, and added the sharp edges to their bows and trained in close range combat. The advantage you thought you had, you don't.

Before the assassin can say anything, Crystal presses her attack using the bow as if it where two swords combined at the hilt, slashing and stabbing at the assassin. The assassin caught of guard by the lethalness of the bow, and the sudden fury of Crystal's attacks is barely able to block or dodge the attacks and is eventually pushed against a large tree. As Crystal comes in with a horizontal slash from right to left at the assassin's waist level, the assassin quickly jumps up into the tree he was up against and the blade of the bow passes through the area where the assassin should have been, scaring the tree instead. Crystal leaps into the air at the same time the assassin lands on a branch in the tree. Using the cutting edge of her bow, Crystal slashes straight through the branch that the assassin lands on, causing him to tumble to the ground, and land face first. After severing the branch, using her free hand, Crystal grabs the branch above her, while posting her feet against the truck of the tree, angling at the assassin she lets go of the branch, while simultaneously pushing off the truck of the tree, she sends herself hurtling towards the assassin with the bow out in front of her intending to impale him with the end of the bow. The assassin getting to his feet and seeing the attack coming moves out of the way of the attack, causing Crystal to change tactics. She loads an arrow while still in flight and launches it at the assassin, who blocks the arrow by twirling his nun-chucks in a circular motion. As Crystal nears the ground she places her shooting hand out in front of her, and as her hand makes contact with the ground she bends her arm at the elbow then using all the strength she has, she flips up to her feet, in time to block a vertical attack from one of the assassin's nun-chucks then she has to immediately block at horizontal strike from her left side. Using her bow, she blocks the attack with the lower half of the bow, the turns the block into a counter attack with the upper portion of the bow, which the assassin ducks under. As the assassin straightens from his avoidance with Crystal's bow, he back flips away from her to create some distance, which Crystal closes in a matter of seconds, with a vertical slash from low to high meant to separate the left half of his body from his right half. As the attack comes closer the assassin sidesteps to his right to avoid the blow, while counter attacking with a horizontal strike to Crystal's chest with the nun-chucks in his left hand. Crystal, having put all her momentum forward, is unable to avoid the attack to her chest by the assassin. The attack while powerful, only knocks her back a few steps and drives the wind from her lungs. Seeing an opportunity, the assassin closes the distance to attack again. Seeing the attack coming, Crystal leaps into a tree, while loading an arrow into her bow, shoots it at the assassin, who deflects it with his nun-chucks, and leaps into the tree after Crystal. Seeing the attacking assassin coming at her, she leaps from the tree towards the assassin in a head to head attack. As the two near each other, they attack with their respective weapons, Crystal with a horizontal slash in front of her head, while the assassin attacks with a low to high attack with both of his nun-chucks. Both of the warriors connect with their attacks, however, Crystal having the added advantage of both gravity and her weapon having a blade, kills the assassin, and even before she lands on the ground the assassin vanishes into nothingness.

As the assassin leaps at Joseph, Joseph takes a different approach and launches himself into the air at the assassin. As they approach one another, their swords meet in a thunderous clash, driving them apart. They land on the ground ten feet from each other, with their weapons up in guard positions.

Assassin(starting a circular motion with Joseph)- Your stronger than I thought. This will be my greatest triumph.

Joseph(grinning)- Don't bet on it. It'll take more than you to take me down.

Without waiting for a reply, Joseph charges the assassin, and leaping into the air and coming down in a flying side kick, that connects with the assassin's head, knocking him to the ground. Not wasting a single moment, Joseph closes the distance with the assassin laying on his back, and leaping again into the air, reverses his grip on his swords coming down above the assassin attempting to drive his blades through the assassin's chest. A split second before Joseph lands the assassin rolls out of the way and springs to his feet and charges Joseph swinging both his blades in a horizontal motion from right to left. Joseph seeing the attack coming, blocks the two incoming swords with the sword in his left hand, while simultaneously performing a horizontal slash of his own with the blade in his right hand. The assassin, seeing the attack coming, barely manages to disengage and leap back away from his enemy in time to avoid a slash that would have killed him. Joseph following up his attack, rushes in attacking with a roundhouse kick from his right leg that connects with the left side of the assassin's face. The assassin is sent spinning to the ground from the shear force of the kick. Joseph again attempts to impale the assassin and is rewarded with the assassin's left foot to his abdomen. Stumbling backwards from the kick, Joseph finds himself gasping for air, as the assassin rises to his feet. As Joseph regains his breath the assassin charges him, attacking with two slashes at the same time, one horizontal, one vertical. Seeing the attacks coming, Joseph blocks both at the same time, and after the blocks have been done, he attacks first with the sword that blocked the vertical strike, and then follows with the sword the blocked the horizontal attack. Both attacks land and draw blood from the assassin, with the second striking just a few inches below the first. The assassin leaps away from Joseph, looking down at his chest and abdomen, seeing the blood leaking from the wounds and seeing the two swords in Joseph's hand stained with his red blood. Joseph seeing a moment of opportunity charges in and while reversing the grip on the sword in his right hand and bringing the blade of that sword against his arm, leaps into the air and comes down with a blade enhanced elbow strike, which the assassin barely manages to avoid by diving into a forward shoulder roll. As Joseph lands, the assassin spins around and attacks. Joseph, using the same tactic as the assassin, does a forward shoulder roll to avoid the attack. Letting the roll carry him to his feet, Joseph quickly spins to face his opponent, and sees the assassin charging him. The assassin, leaps into the air, performing a half flip so that he is pointing directly at Joseph, and extending his blades he starts to hurtle down at him, in an attempt to impale Joseph with his blades. Joseph seeing the attack coming moves out of the way, and as the assassin lands, charges him while performing two vertical slashes, one from high to low, the other low to high, however, the assassin manages to dodge them.

Assassin(breathing heavily)- I'm impressed, but it is time to end this. DARK FLAME SLASH!!!!!!!!!!!!!

As the assassin comes rushing at Joseph, his swords become engulfed in black flames as he slashes several times at Joseph. Joseph seeing how lethal the attack the assassin is using, goes strictly defensive and manages to deflect or dodge each slash, to the surprise of the assassin.

Joseph- That's not a bad attack, but, for it to be effective, you have to actually hit your enemy, which you didn't do. Now it's my turn. FLAME SLASH ATTACK!!!!!!!!!!!!!!!!!

Calling on a power identical to the one that the assassin used in every way except, instead of his swords being engulfed in black flames, they're engulfed in white flames. Charging in and attacking with a speed that the assassin can't even begin to match, Joseph *connects with four slash attacks, two from each flame engulfed blade. The first strikes across the assassin's chest, the second connects with the abdomen, the third slashes the assassin through the waist, and final slash removes the assassin's head. Even before the head hits the ground, the three pieces vanish into the void of non-existence. As Joseph resheathes his blades the other three warriors come out of the forest.*

Joseph (looking at everyone in turn)- Everyone alright.

Kim, Kenneth, and Crystal- Yeah.

Kim (stepping up to Joseph)- How about you, are you okay?

Joseph- I'm fine, let's get moving, we're not too far from the top.

Joseph, leads the others the rest of the way up the mountain. As they near the top, Joseph sees the three creatures that Kim had told them all about and steels himself for the coming battles.

All creatures- be warned, if you did not come with tribute, you will either leave or fight. If you fight, you will most certainly die.

Joseph(stepping forward)- We didn't come all this way to die, but, we can't turn back now, to much is at stake. I humbly ask that you allow us to pass, otherwise, we will have to fight and one of us will have to die.

Creatures(standing as still as stones)- You bring no tribute, yet you say you cannot turn back. There is no choice, we fight. Choose you champion from your group, but, choose wisely.

Joseph- I shall be the one to fight.

Creatures- Very well, you will be allowed one substitute at anytime during any of the three battles; however, once the substitute has been made, it cannot be undone, do you understand.

Joseph(nodding his head)- Yes I do.

Creatures- Then prepare yourself.

Joseph(spreading his feet shoulder width apart and crossing his arms across his chest)- ARMOR OF SHINOBI, IGNITE!!!!!!!!!!!!!!!!!!

After Joseph summons his armor he draws his swords, and stands ready for the first of three battles to begin. The first of the battles begins with the creature made of earth. The creature charges Joseph with surprising speed. As it draws near, Joseph quickly leaps over the creature doing a twisting flip, to come down behind and facing the creature, and as he lands, he slices through the creature, and it's upper body falls to the ground.

Joseph (resheathing his swords)- Well that was easier than I thought it would be.

As Joseph turns to face his next opponent, he hears a very disturbing sound. He turns back to see where the creature had been laying and sees that the bottom half of the creature is standing upright, and that the upper half of it's body was reattaching itself to the lower half through the use of vines. As the creature literally pulls itself together, Joseph stands there in amazement, wondering how he can defeat this opponent. The creature, now fully restored to it's normal state charges Joseph once again, but this time as it nears, it attacks with a right handed thrust punch meant for Joseph's head. Joseph quickly deflects the attack with a block from his left hand and sidesteps to the left and delivers a vicious right hand of his own to the creatures rib cage and is rewarded with a satisfying crunch. As the two separate, Joseph sees that the damage inflicted to the creature is already repairing itself. Not seeing any other choice, Joseph draws his swords and rushes in to attack the creature again. Bringing his blades in a slashing movement, one from either side, Joseph attacks the creature, however, the creature sees the attack coming and stomps his right foot on the ground and two blade length pieces of wood shoot up into his hands and the creature blocks both of his swords and counters with simultaneous strikes to either side of Joseph's body. Leaping into the air and driving his feet into the creature's chest Joseph flips backwards, while pushing the creature back away from him at the same time, creating some much needed distance. The creature closes the distance to press it's advantage, and attacks with the fighting sticks in it's hands. The creature attacks with a horizontal slashing motion to the right side of Joseph's head, aimed at the temple, while with the stick in it's left hand attacks the rib cage with another horizontal slash. After blocking both attacks with his blades, Joseph sends the creature to the ground with a furious thrust kick to the creatures left knee. Trying to capitalize on his advantage Joseph leaps into the air, attempting to drive his feet through the creatures chest on impact, however, the creature manages to get both of his feet to his chest and catching Joseph foot on foot, throws him backwards into a large tree truck. After Joseph impacts against the tree, he falls face first to the ground, but, manages to get to his feet quick enough to avoid the next attack, a furious punch meant to leave an imprint of the creatures fist in his face. Joseph avoids the attack by moving his head to the left, and the creature's fist impacts against the tree. As the creature retracts it's fist, Joseph doubles him over with a knee strike to his stomach, then sends him flying through the air with a leaping knee strike to the face, again creating some distance between the two. As the creature flies through the air, Joseph notices what looks like tree roots reaching up to the creature in an attempt to catch the creature. Seeing where the creature draws it's amazing strength, Joseph looks around the battle area for something that he can use to pin the creature to, and is rewarded with the sight of a giant boulder. Joseph rushes in at the creature with wild slashes meant to drive the creature back towards the boulder, and as he nears it, Joseph knocks creature into the air a powerful side kick, and as the creature hit the boulder, Joseph stabs his swords through the creature penning him to the boulder, then quickly stepping back, Joseph unleashes the power of the shinobi blast, incinerating any roots that come up from the ground to heal or strengthen the creature until it withers and dies. Joseph walks to where the creatures now dead body hangs, and removes his swords from the creature's body, and as it falls to the ground Joseph sheathes both of his swords and turns to the remaining two creatures.

Creatures (still standing as still as statues)- Well done. You are the first to defeat our brother in combat, now you must face another.

Joseph (taking a deep breath and stepping forward)- If this must be done, than let it be done. Which one of you will I be fighting next.

The creature made of stone steps forward, and brings it hands together in front of Joseph.

Creature made of stone (as it steps forward)- I am your next opponent. May the best warrior win.

The second battle begins, and with a baffling speed, the stone creature charges at Joseph. Joseph avoids being bowled over by leaping over the creature and as he passes it manages to land a kick to the back of the creatures head, sending it tumbling head over heels into the ground. As Joseph lands, he once again draws his swords knowing that his fists, won't be any match for the stone creatures brute strength. The creature climbs back to its feet, and charges Joseph once again, but, this time it attacks with a wild hook punch with its right hand that Joseph ducks under and then moves to his left out of its way, simultaneously slashing across the creatures abdomen with the sword in his right hand. Even though Joseph connects with his attack, he barely leaves a scratch on the stone body of the creature. As Joseph is noticing the almost, nonexistent damage he has done to the creature, it turns its upper body and connects with a backhanded fist to the side of Joseph's head, sending him spinning on a three foot flight through the air to land hard on his back. As Joseph gets to his feet he tastes his own blood in his mouth, and spits some of it out. Joseph charges at the creature, and as he nears it leaps into the air performing a front flip to land with his feet, knees bent, *against a tree, that he pushes off of to gain more speed for his next attack. Diving through the air at the creature, Joseph slashes with both swords at the head and chest of the creature, not only leaving deeper scratches in the creatures stone body this time, but, also taking the creature off of its feet, and sending him sliding along the ground for a good five feet. As Joseph lands on the ground a couple of feet from where the creature had been standing, the creature slowly makes it way to its feet, surprised by the power of the attack that was just used against it.*

Stone creature (getting up from the ground)- You impress me again, you are the first to knock me from my feet, something not easily done.

Joseph (breathing heavily and taking a defensive stance)- thanks for the compliment, but, I'm still unsure as to how I'm gonna beat you. I thought I might be able to hack you pieces with my blades, but, that would take too much time, time I don't have, but, I have to figure something out.

Without replying the stone creature charges Joseph, and this time it's Joseph's turn to be impressed by the creature. As it nears Joseph, it leaps an easy twenty feet into the air, intending to use its own body mass as the instrument of Joseph's defeat and death. Seeing what the creature has in mind, Joseph dashes out of the way of the incoming creature and jumps towards a tree, and while still in mid air, turns so his feet land against the tree. Pushing off of the tree, Joseph again sends himself hurtling at the creature, but, instead of attacking with his blades, he drives both of his feet into the chest of the creature sending it hurtling backwards and through a tree directly behind it. As the creature hits the ground it slides another five feet and comes to rest against a small boulder. After the creature gets to its feet, it moves behind the small boulder it was just up against, and lifts it into the air and sends it flying towards Joseph. Seeing the boulder coming, Joseph dives for the ground as the small boulder passes by harmlessly over his head. Climbing to his feet, Joseph feels an urgent need to end the battle, so throwing caution to the wind, he charges the stone creature.

Joseph (while charging at the stone creature)- LIGHTNING TRIPLE STRIKE!!!!!

As Joseph closes the distance to the creature he strikes with two horizontal strikes to the stomach and chest of the creature and a vertical strike to the head of the stone menace, and after each strike a bolt of lightning hits the creature in every area that his blades touched, causing the creature to explode into tiny pieces. As Joseph turns to face his third and final opponent he notices that this one is a little different in appearance. This one looks more human than the other two. Wearing cloths as red as blood, and it's face covered by a black mask with only eyes as red a fire showing through the mask, and a cape blacker than night.

Creature (walking forward towards Joseph, igniting fireballs in it's hands)- You a truly a rare opponent; but now you face the strongest of the three brothers, your death is certain.

Before Joseph can even reply to the creature, Kim starts walking forward with her armor starting to appear on her body out of thin air, and with a look of grim determination on her face.

Kim (walking towards the creature)- To bad for you, he's not your opponent, I am.

Joseph (surprise and dismay showing on his face)- Kim, what are you doing, I can handle this fight.

Kim (looking over to Joseph)- I know you can, but I have a score to settle with this creature. He's the one that burned my village to the ground.

Joseph (nodding his head, and backing away)- I understand, but, a piece of advice, don't let you anger get the better of you.

Kim (looking back at the creature)- I won't.

Creature (stepping towards his new opponent)- So you where the one that Ryan wanted, a pity, I would have rather killed you with the rest of your village.

Kim- That will never happen, and after today, their souls will be able to rest in peace.

Not giving her enemy a chance to reply, Kim charges in and draws her swords, and attacks with a double slashing motion. The creature leaps above the two incoming swords and throws two fireballs at Kim, knocking her back and to the ground a good ten feet. Not allowing herself a moments rest after the attack, Kim leaps to her feet and rushes towards her enemy, dodging the constant barge of fireballs being hurled at her. As she nears the creature she ducks low, and then lungs up at the creature driving her right knee into the creatures abdomen, not only doubling him over, but, sending him hurtling through the air. Not wasting a single moment, she leaps into the air coming down on top of the creature, driving her swords into his chest. As Kim stands up to her full height, she removes her swords from the form of the creature. As she sheathes her blade and starts to walk away, the creature silently gets back up and throw a fireball at the back of her head that sends her face first into the ground. Climbing back to her feet, she looks at the creature and assumes a defensive posture.

Kim (confusion on her face)- How did you survive that, you should be dead.

Creature (chuckling softly)- I can't be beaten that easily, your swords can't kill me.

Kim (determination returning to her face)- Well, I'll just have to kill you another way.

Without replying the creature charges at Kim, driving his right knee into her stomach, doubling her over, and then connecting with a fireball enhanced uppercut to her face, sending her flying several feet through the air to come crashing down on her back. Leaping up to her feet Kim dashes in toward the creature, dodging and deflecting fireballs as she goes. As she get nearer, she notices that one of the fireballs she sent back at the creature connected and caused him a great amount of pain. Seeing that the use of his own power against him might be her only chance at defeating him, she continues to deflect his fireball back towards him, gaining accuracy with each fireball she deflects. As the creature sees her strategy, he starts to dodge the fireballs that she is deflecting back towards him. As she draws nearer, he notices that the armor she is wearing has changed ever so slightly at the hands. She closed her fingers together and the armor around them has became one piece instead of five, allowing her the ability to deflect the fireballs he was throwing at her. As she closes the distance, the creature enhances his hands in flames in preparation for hand to hand combat, however, he notices another slight difference in the armor that Kim is wearing, the area where the armor changed to allow her to deflect his fireballs is also razor sharp. As Kim reaches the creature she starts thrusting and slashing motions with her hands, which her enemy manages to deflect or dodge. As the exchange continues, she catches him on the side of the head with an unexpected roundhouse kick, which puts five feet of distance between them. As she charges at him again he resumes his barge of fireballs. As she continues moving towards her opponent, Kim continues to deflect as many fireballs as she can back at him, even though he dodges most of them. When she closes to within a few feet of the creature, she deflects three fireballs in a row, sending them back at him with such speed that he can't get out of the way in time, and is hit by all three. As the last fireball strikes his chest, his body starts to glow a bright orange-red, until, the very flames that empowered him become his demise, engulfing and incinerating him to nothing. As Kim finishes her battle, night is starting to descend on the area, and the four warriors decide to set up camp on the top of the mountain.

Joseph (moving over to Kim)- You fought well, (addressing the rest of the group)we should set camp a quick

as possible. Kenneth, Crystal, I'm leaving you to two to set things up here, Kim and I are gonna go get some wood to get a fire going.

Kenneth (turning towards Crystal)- I guess we should get started then.

Joseph (facing Kim again)- Let's go.

As Kenneth and Crystal set up the camp, Joseph and Kim leave to collect the wood to build a fire. As the two of them are traveling through the woods, Joseph starts to talk to Kim.

Joseph (picking up a piece of wood)- So you got your revenge.

Kim (sounding subdued)- Yeah, it's funny, I thought I would feel better.

Joseph (turning and looking down into Kim's eyes)- Hate can never make a person feel better, even after gaining vengeance. I think this will be enough wood, let's head back to camp.

After the two return to the camp the warriors eat and then get some sleep after a very tiresome day.

CHAPTER EIGHT

THE LAKE AND A
NEW FRIEND

As the light of the next morning wakes the four warriors and friends, Kim goes over to look over the last stretch, to the island, where the evil being waits within, the one who Joseph will have to face and defeat. As she turns to go pack her supplies, she notices someone climbing up the hardest portion of the mountain to climb, the straight vertical face. Upon seeing this unexpected guest she runs over to Joseph.

Kim (grabbing Joseph and pulling him to the edge of the mountain)- Joseph, there is someone there, do you see him, climbing the vertical face.

Kenneth (looking over at Kim)- Kim, that is vertical face, it's damn near impossible to climb.

Joseph (looking back to Kenneth and hooking a thumb over his shoulder)- Tell that to him.

As Kim and Joseph step back from the edge of the mountain, Kenneth starts over towards them to see what or who they have been talking about, but, doesn't even make it five steps before a man of medium build, with dirty blonde hair, and black eyes pulls himself up over the mountain to stand right in front of them, panting and sweating like a pig.

Stranger (breathing heavily and wiping sweat off of his brow)- Hey, how are you guys?

Joseph (stepping forward cautiously)- We're fine. Who are you, and if you don't mind me asking, why were you climbing the mountain when there was a path right over there(pointing to the path to the right of the new comer).

Stranger (slapping himself on the forehead with the palm of his hand)- Damn, I knew I forgot something. Oh yeah (smiling sheepishly) my name is Tim. As for why I was climbing the mountain, no reason. Ahh, who are you guys?

Joseph (pointing to each in turn)- I'm Joseph, that's Kenneth, then there is Crystal, and finally Kim, who was the first of our group to see you climbing the mountain. Now, not to seem rude, but, we have to be on our way.

The four start on their way down the side of the mountain that Tim came up, via the path. As they start down the path, Tim stops them.

Tim (smiling again)- Are you guys going down to the lake.

Joseph (stopping and turning to face Tim)- Yes and to the island in the center of it.

Tim (still smiling)- I hope you guys were not planning to try to swim across the lake. If you were I would think otherwise, you wouldn't survive the swim.

Joseph- Why's that?

Tim (bringing his right hand up with two fingers extended)- Two reasons, first, you would need special equipment to survive it, which, from the looks of it, you don't have, that water is pretty pullulated, only a few things have been able to adapt to it and survive without the use of the special equipment I mentioned. The second is there is a legend. One of the creatures that has adapted to living in there is a merman, but, because of the pollution in the water, he went insane. Anyone that he finds swimming or even boating on that lake, with the exception of the Black Shinobi he attacks, and most don't survive to tell the tale. The fact is that it is more than a legend, I've seen the merman before. If I were you I would turn back now and forget about whatever it is you are trying to do.

Joseph (looking down and shaking his head)- Unfortunately, we don't have that luxury. We'll have to make some sort of raft or something to get us across

Tim- Do any of you know how to make a raft.

All four of the warriors look down while shaking their heads.

Well lucky for you guys, I do, and I can make one for you, so, let's get moving.

The five make their way down the mountain with Tim in the lead, Crystal and Kenneth behind him, and Joseph and Kim bringing up the rear. As the five walk Kim notices that Tim is acting a little strangely, walking like a gorilla, swinging on vines, jumping through the trees, and performing acrobatics, for no apparent reason. As the five continue their Journey, Joseph notices the look of concern on Kim's face as she watches Tim.

Joseph (looking over at Kim)- Are you alright?

Kim (looking back at Joseph and thinking before she says anything)- I'm fine, but..........

Joseph (cutting Kim off)- You're worried about our guide. You think he might be insane.

Kim (looking away from Joseph)- Yeah.

Joseph (looking back at Tim)- I've been watching him like you have, and I can tell you now, he's not insane, he acting like he is.

Kim (looking up at Joseph with curiosity in her eyes)- How do you know?

Joseph (looking back at Kim with a smile on his face)- Think about it. When we were on top of the mountain, he was talking clearly, thinking clearly, no sign of insanity, it wasn't until we started moving down here that he started acting this way. My thoughts is that he doesn't want anyone to mess with him, so he acts like he is insane so people will leave him alone either out of pity or fear. He is smarter than he lets on.

As the five continue to move, Tim hears Joseph and Kim talking about him in the rear of the group and the concern Kim feels for their guide. Without warning, Tim leaps straight into a tree and leaps towards Joseph and Kim and lands right in front of them in a crouch, putting Kim on guard immediately.

Tim (coming up to his true height)- Relax Kim, if I wanted to harm you, I would have already done so. I heard you two talking. Your very observant Joseph and right. I'm not insane. I've been acting like this for the past four days.

Kim (cautiously moving towards Tim)- Why, I don't understand why you would.

Tim (lifting his right hand to show a mark of a dragon on it)- You and I are from the same village Kim. I left long ago, but, I still had family and friends there. When I heard what Ryan had done there, I raced to the village to see if I could find anyone still left alive, I wasn't able to get there in time, I thought all of them were dead, then I heard a rumor that one survived, because Ryan wanted her as his bride. I managed to sneak by the guardians of the mountain and was trying to figure a way to get to the island and try to rescue you, but, after everything I saw, I knew I wasn't strong enough, so I started to go back to find help. Now I see you somehow managed to get away from him, and have made some powerful friends. All I care about now is bringing Ryan down, putting an end to his evil.

Joseph (stepping towards Tim)- I can see how committed you are to this, and we can always use another friend and ally.

Joseph steps back from Tim and summons his armor, then steps again towards Tim and draws his swords.

Joseph- Take a knee.

As Tim kneels down, Joseph touches him on his shoulders with each blade, and Kenneth is engulfed in white flames, as the flames die down, Tim emerges in a white armor, with some differences from the others. On the pieces to cover his arms and feet, there are adjustable armor pieces that act like fins, making him capable of underwater movement and fighting. The helmet he wears is different as well in a minor way, yet the adjustment is just as important. The face mask when pulled down and in place allows him to see and breathe underwater, making it possible for him to stay in the water for hours at a time. The last noticeable difference is that the helmet has one razor sharp fin curving back on the top of it.

Joseph (looking down at Tim while he sheathes his swords)- Welcome to the group. Now, lets get to the shore, build this raft, and get to that island.

Tim (looking up grinning)- Lets do it.

The five warriors rush to the shore. When they get there, Tim instructs them on what he needs to make a raft to get them across. The items come to logs, vines, strong branches, something to use as a sail, and finally a prayer for wind. Joseph, using his swords cut the trees down, and then cuts the branches from them. As Joseph and Tim lay the newly made logs next to each other, Kim uses the vines she cut from trees in the forest to bind them together. Crystal using the blades of her bow, leaps throw the trees to find and cut branches strong enough to serve as the mast of a sail, and Kenneth, using the spike in the end of his three sectional staff, makes a deep enough grove in the raft to place the mast securely. As the raft comes near to completion the only thing missing is the sail.

Joseph (looking at everyone in turn)- Anyone have anything we can use for a sail?

Kim (moving to her bag and looking through it)- I have something. It was given to me by my mother. It should work.

After Kim finishes digging through her bag, she produces an old blanket, one that she had obviously for years. It was a white as pure snow, and in the center was etched the image of a gold dragon. Walking over to Joseph, she places it in his hands.

Joseph (pushing the blanket back into Kim's hands)- Kim I can't take this, I know it has to have a lot of sentimental value to you, I don't want it to be destroyed.

Kim (taking the blanket in her hands, and walking over to the mast)- We don't have a choice, we need a sail, and I doubt anyone else has something that can be used. Besides, I always knew this blanket was special, that it was meant for something important, and I think I know what that is now. I believe it is meant to announce the return of the White Shinobi Clan.

Without further argument from Joseph or anyone else, Kim fastens the blanket to the mast. As she does so, the other four warriors watch silently behind them, knowing what she is doing is announcing that a light to the world that has been in hiding has returned to destroy a great darkness. As she finishes fastening it to the mast, the other four warriors push the raft into the water and board, with Tim at the front of the raft, Joseph and Kim sitting under the banner of the White Shinobi Clan, and Kenneth and Crystal taking up the rear of the raft.

Joseph (looking into Kim's eyes and taking her hand in his)- Thank you for this, and I promise it will not be forgotten.

Kim (looking into Joseph's eyes)- I know, and your welcome.

As the raft continues to drift across the lake to their final destination, the five warriors contemplate in silence everything that has happened to bring them to this point, and all of them know that they are ready to make the ultimate sacrifice to end the evil that is infecting the world. After two hours the raft nears the halfway point on the journey to the island that the final battle will take place at; however, Tim sees something leap out of the water at a distance.

Tim (standing up and focusing on the image in the distance)- Guys I think trouble Just found us.

Crystal (moving up to stand next to Tim)- What do you mean?

Just then the merman leaps out of the water, and in his right hand is a unique looking sword. The hilt looks as though it is made of a long dead fish with the blade extending from its mouth.

Tim (turning to face everyone)- My armor is meant to fight in the water, so, I'll take care of this one.

Before anyone can argue Tim turns, summons his armor, and leaps into the water. As his body disappears under the water's surface, the fins on his armor lock into place above his hands and feet, and the only thing anyone above the water can see is a huge object speeding away from the raft as if it were a torpedo. As Tim speeds through the water with the speed of a dolphin, he draws the two pieces of his weapon, a trident, and combines them, placing them in his right hand. As he continues moving through the water, the merman comes up from under him attempting to impale him on his sword; however, Tim rolls up onto his left side, causing the sword to connect with a grazing blow with the dull side of the weapon. As Tim alters his course the merman continues with his upward momentum to leap out of the water, and while in midair, turns his body so he re-enters the water head first. As he enters the water, it becomes the merman's turn to avoid being run through by Tim's trident. Moving too fast to avoid contact, the merman, blocks the trident being used to attack him, by knocking it to the right side of his body and then after the block swings his sword at Tim's head. Tim, seeing the attack coming, quickly propels himself onto his right side so that the sword passes harmlessly past his head, while kicking out with his left foot to strike the merman in the ribcage, causing him to let out a gurgled scream of pain. As the merman screams in pain, he swims off into the darkness of the water, to come back at Tim from a completely different angle, striking him with his tail and moving him through the water several feet. Using the momentum of the strike by the merman's tail, Tim swims into the darkness of the water himself and turns. Unable to see were the merman is, Tim starts a full speed swim, hoping that his enemy in still in the same place as he left him, and as he draws nearer to that place he sees that the merman had the same idea as he did, finding himself in a head to head charge. As the two draw nearer to each other the merman positions his sword for a horizontal slash in front of his head, while Tim readies his trident for his counter. When the two get within striking distance of each other, the merman executes his horizontal slash, while Tim starts his counter. To the merman's horror, Tim anticipated the merman's attack, and using his trident, caught and trapped the sword, and with a swift movement, Tim disarms the merman, while at the same time striking at the merman's abdomen with the blunt end of his trident, doubling him over, and knocking him several feet away from himself. The merman, seeing his sword vanishing into the darkness of the lake, speeds away to retrieve it before he can no longer see it. Moving at a speed so fast that he looks like a blur, the merman, manages to catch his sword before it vanishes into the depths of the darkness of the lake, then maintaining his speed, he charges through the water at Tim in a blind rage. Tim seeing the insanity in his opponent's eyes, stops and brings himself upright in the water, then brings his trident straight in front of him, holding it vertically, in preparation for his strongest attack.

Tim (twirling his trident in several figure eight patterns in front of him)- TSUNAMI STRIKE!!!!!!!!!!!!!!!!!!!!!!!!!!!

Locking his trident into his right side after the several figure eight patterns and gathering the energy from the water moving around him, Tim thrust his trident forward, and a tsunami of pure energy races through the water, striking the merman in his chest, and killing him on contact. As the lifeless corpse drifts towards the bottom of the lake, the merman's remains start to dissolve into nothingness, leaving not even a skeleton to prove his existence.

With the battle over, Tim swims to the surface of the water. As he breaks the surface, he looks around for his comrades, and sees' that they are near the sure. Putting on a burst of speed, Tim torpedoes himself through the water to catch up with the raft. As he nears it he sees a hand extend to help him onto the raft. Once aboard the raft, the others congratulate Tim on his victory. Shortly after that, the raft makes it to shore, and the five warriors disembark and begin the final part of their journey to their destiny.

CHAPTER NINE

THE ISLAND OF THE BLACK SHINOBI

As the five warriors walk up the shore of the island, they find themselves staring at a dense forest, directly in front of them.

Kim (looking at the forest)- This is, next to the Black Shinobi Temple, the most dangerous part of our journey. The temple rests in the center of the forest. That is where the final battle will be held, and where you (now looking directly at Joseph) Joseph, have a date with destiny.

Joseph (looking at the forest then turning to face the others)- No matter what happens there today, I want you all to know that it has been my greatest honor to know all of you, and to call each of you a friend. Now, let's finish this.

The five comrades head into the forest not knowing what awaits them, but, knowing that no matter what happens they cannot fail in the coming battle. Two hours into the journey, Tim slows his pace so that he is right beside Kim and Joseph.

Tim (looking at Kim)- Kim, would mind if I talked with Joseph alone for a few moments?

Kim (picking up her pace)- Not at all.

Joseph (waiting till Kim is out of listening range)- So Tim, what's on your mind?

Tim (looking over at Joseph)- To be honest, you are.

Joseph (now looking at Tim with a curious look)- What do you mean?

Tim- Joseph, how do you feel about Kim?

Joseph (visibly caught off guard by Tim's question)- Tim, this isn't the time or the place to be talking about such things.

Tim- That is where you are wrong, after today, there may never be another time or place to talk about this.

Joseph- You're not gonna let this go, are you?

Tim- Not till you give me an answer.

Joseph (letting out a sigh)- Alright, I'll tell you. I love her, but, I can't afford to think about it right now, I have to stay focused on what I have to do, destroying the evil that the Black Shinobi Clan represents.

Tim- I understand that better then you think, but, not allowing yourself to feel, can hurt you as well.

Joseph- I understand that, but, right now is not the time to tell her, we don't know what will happen, but, I will do everything I can to protect her, that way when it is done, I'll have a chance to tell her.

Tim (letting out a sigh of his own)- I hope you get the chance to tell her, I'd hate for you to have to live with not being able to tell her for the rest of your life.

Joseph (putting his hand on Tim's shoulder)- I would hate that too.

As Tim and Joseph finish their conversation, they pick up the pace to close the gap that had been created between them and the others, and as they draw closer, Tim and Kim take up their original positions. Another hour passes, and the five comrades find themselves in a clearing, where a lone figure waits in the center. The lone figure is the same height as Joseph, but, has a slightly larger build. He has short, black hair and eyes. His skin has a dark tan to it, and his clothes are torn in different places, and the final thing that can be noticed about this man is that he carries two hooked swords, one over his left shoulder, and the other over his right shoulder.

Joseph (taking a cautious step forward)- Are you alright?

Unknown man (drawing his swords)- I'm fine, it's you who are in trouble.

Before Joseph can even say anything in response to this, this stranger charges him and attacks with both of his swords, in a double horizontal slash from either side of Joseph's body, causing Joseph to leap into the air and over this new enemy. As he lands he turns to face his opponent, while at the same time summons his twin katanas.

Joseph (stepping into a fighting stance)- I don't know who you are, or why your attacking me, but, I have no time to play around with you.

Without saying another word, or wasting a single movement Joseph goes on the attack with a diagonal slash attack meant to cut his opponent from left shoulder to right hip; however, his enemy dodges it and attacks with a vertical strike meant to cut Joseph in half from head to groin. Joseph seeing the attack coming parries it to the left with the sword in his left hand while attacking with a horizontal strike from right to left. His opponent blocks with his left sword, with the curved tip pointing to the ground. Joseph seeing an opening, thrusts his right foot into his enemy's stomach, sending him back a couple of feet, and doubling him over. Joseph presses his advantage by getting in close and landing a vertical knee to his unknown enemy's face. As his knee connects, Joseph feel the cartridge in his opponent's nose give way and break. The unknown man goes flying up into the air, only to land hard with a thud on his back. As the man gets to his feet, he wipes away the blood coming from his broken nose with the back of his right hand and looks down at it.

Unknown man (still looking at his hand)- You're the first to make me bleed, you'll pay for this.

Going into a blind rage the unknown man charges Joseph, swinging his blades wildly. Joseph, because of his enemy's rage, is able to see the attacks even before his enemy throws them, thus enabling him to dodge them with ease. On one of the unknown man's attacks, Joseph sidesteps, and then connects with a round kick to the side of his opponents head, sending him to the ground with a loud thud.

Joseph (bring his swords up in front of him)- It's time I ended this.

Unknown man (getting to his feet, glaring at Joseph)- YOU WON'T WIN!!!!!!!!!!!!!!!!!!!!!!!!!!!!!!

The unknown man charges blindly at Joseph and as he get near attacks with the same double slash he used in the beginning of the fight, Joseph seeing this, avoids it the same way, however, while in mid-air, Joseph twists so that when he lands he is facing his enemy's back, and finishes him off with a double horizontal slash of his own removing his enemy's head.

Joseph (letting his swords vanish to rejoin his armor and turning to look at his friends)- This battle has ended, let's get to the temple.

The five warriors rush from the clearing back into the dense forest, heading to the temple, where the final battle will take place.

CHAPTER TEN

THE FINAL
CONFRONTATION

As the five warriors come to the center of the forest of the island, Joseph calls for a stop.

Joseph (in front of everyone else, raising his hand to stop the others)- Kenneth, you seem to know the most about this, is there a way inside besides the front door?

Kenneth (now beside Joseph)- There might be. Legend has it that there is a secret door that only a White Shinobi Master can open.

Joseph (looking Kenneth in the eyes)- Where?

Kenneth (covering his chin in a thinking posture)- If I remember correctly, it should be somewhere along the back of the temple.

Joseph (turning to face everyone)- Alright, we'll move through the forest to the back side of the temple, and then we'll start searching for the secret way in and hope that the legend is true about it.

The five move through the forest, and five minutes later they find themselves at the back of the temple, and discover that there is no security there. Seeing this Joseph immediately sends his friends and comrades to search different areas of the temple backside. As the other four spread out over the areas that they are to search, Joseph heads to the section that he left for himself and begins his search. As the five are searching their areas of the temple, Joseph's hand brushes up against a stone in the temple. At his touch the stone illuminates causing Joseph to jump back a couple of feet. The others seeing this out of the corner of their eyes rush over to where Joseph is standing.

Kim (getting to Joseph first)- Are you okay?

Joseph (turning to look at her)- I'm fine. I think I might have just found the secret entrance.

Kenneth (stepping closer to Joseph)- You're the only one it will react to. Let me try, which stone did you touch.

Joseph (pointing to a stone)- That one there.

Kenneth (placing his hand against the stone, nothing happens)- Well, I think this is it.

Joseph steps up to the stone again and places his hand on it. As he touches the stone, it begins to glow again, and as he places his entire hand against it, the glowing grows brighter to the point of blinding them, then all at once it just disappears and the black block that was there is replaced by a white block with the dragon of the White Shinobi Clan imprinted on it, the same dragon that is imprinted on Joseph's armor.

Joseph (stepping back from the stone)- I have a feeling I need my armor to open this door.

Wasting no time Joseph summons his armor, and after it appears on him, the dragon on his chest plate starts to glow, shining a bright light at the dragon on the stone. As the dragon on the stone starts to illuminate, a whole section of stones begin to disappear, giving the warriors their entrance. As the five begin to enter the temple their way is barred by five warriors clad in from head to toe in black armor.

Joseph (shaking his head)- I should have known it wasn't gonna be that easy.

Armored man 1 (stepping forward)- I'm Brian, second in command of the Black Shinobi Clan, surrender now and I promise to kill you quick.

Joseph (looking directly at Brian)- Sorry, but, your about die.

Kim (putting a hand on Joseph's chest)- Brian is mine, he and I have some unfinished business.

Brian (looking at Kim)- You don't have the power to beat me girl. Fight me and you will be reunited with your father.

Joseph (looking at Brian and shaking his head)- I have a feeling you just bit off more than you can chew. Tim, Kenneth, Crystal, we'll take care of the others, Kim, Brian is all yours.

Kim (looking over at Joseph)- Thanks.

As Kim starts moving towards Brian her armor starts to appear on her in flames licking different parts of her body, and as she moves to draw her twin katanas, her swords appear through flames on her back with the hilts in her hands, and as she draws them her helmet is the last part of her armor to appear. After Kim is adorned in her armor, Crystal, Tim, and Kenneth summon theirs in the usual fashion and as the others attack their enemies, Kim charges Brian.

As Kim nears Brian, she attempts to split him in half with a vertical slash, but, Brian avoids the attack by simply jumping backwards, and as he lands, he draws his own swords. After drawing his swords, Brian surges forward with a sword slash of his own, meant to slash Kim in half from right hip to left hip, however, Kim blocks the attack with the sword in her left hand, while simultaneously performing the same attack that Brian used with the sword in her right hand. Brian, seeing the attack, blocks it with the same movement that Kim used while simultaneously thrusting his right foot into Kim's abdomen, doubling her over. Seeing his advantage, Brian, leaps into the air driving his left knee into Kim's face, sending her through the air several feet to land with a thud on her back. As Brian charges towards Kim, she sits up in time to see him coming, and goes into a backwards somersault to avoid the killing stab of one of Brian's swords. Using the somersault to get to her feet, Kim moves forward and nails Brian in the temple with a roundhouse Kick from her right leg, sending him to the ground spinning. As Brian starts getting to his feet, Kim comes crashing down driving both of her knees into the small of his back and using the forward momentum she developed from the attack to roll forward off of Brian and up to her feet. After Brian gets to his feet, he rushes at Kim. As he gets in close to her he starts stabbing with his two blades as fast as he can in an effort of pierce her armor and kill her, however, Kim, seeing what Brian is trying to do, doesn't even attempt to block the attacks and instead, dodges them, moving closer, to her enemy, and as she gets close enough to where his attacks can't harm her, she attacks, driving the hilt of one of her swords into Brian's jaw, dazing him momentarily. Unfortunately for Brian that one moment of being dazed was all Kim needed. Bringing the sword in her right hand up, she slashes at Brian with a horizontal attack, removing his head from the rest of his body. As the headless corpse falls to the ground she turns seeing that the others have finished their battles as well. As she moves to join her comrades at the entrance she resheathes both of her swords.

Joseph- Is everyone alright?

Kenneth (as everyone else nods)- Yeah.

Joseph (turning to face the entrance)- Good, let's move.

The five warriors enter the dark temple, rushing past several small rooms searching for Ryan. As time passes they eventually find themselves in a large ceremonial room, with three large statues in the form of long dead Black Shinobi Masters. As the five start to leave the room, they hear a noise and turn in it's direction only to discover that the three statues have begun to move towards them, drawing large stone weapons.

Joseph (looking down and shaking his head)- Great, stone guardians. Just what we needed.

Tim- Joseph, you and Kim keep going, the rest of us will handle these three.

Joseph (looking at Tim)- Are you guys sure?

Kenneth- Yeah, we can handle things here. You two find Ryan and take him out.

Kim- You guys be careful.

Crystal (looking back a Joseph and Kim)- Yeah right, now you two GET OUTTA HERE!!!!!!!!!!!!

As Joseph and Kim continue the race to find and defeat Ryan, the other three prepare to square off against the three stone statues. The only thing that distinguishes the statues from one another is the weapons they wield. Kenneth prepares to face off against one that uses a spear, while Tim faces one with a sword, and Crystal prepares to fight one with a staff. The battle begins when the one with the spear thrust it straight at Kenneth, who dodges it by leaping backwards, then leaps onto the spear and dashes up the spear towards the statues head and as he draws near leaps into the air while swinging his three-sectional staff over his head to connects with a strike to the statue's face. Kenneth's leap takes him past the head as he strikes it, and as he lands on the floor he spins around and notices that his attack didn't have any effect on the statue as it turns to face him. As Kenneth prepares to continue his battle, Crystal is in the midst of a furious battle with the staff wielding statue. Crystal is using both long range and short range attacks on her enemy. She shots one arrow after another in rapid succession and as they fall over the target she moves in and attacks with the blades on each end of her bow, landing vertical and horizontal attacks, but, doing little more than scratching the surface of the statue. Meanwhile Tim is dodging and blocking multiple sword slashes from his statue while working his way inside to attack. As he gets close enough he thrusts his trident at the statue, trying to impale the statue on his weapon, but, only having it bounce of the statue leaving a scratch mark. As they all look unbelievingly at the statues and seeing that nothing they are doing has any effect on them, the statues at the same time, attack knocking Tim, Kenneth, and Crystal through the air, to land twenty feet away from them. The three slowly get to their feet, as the statues slowly move in for the kill.

Tim (breathing hard)- What are we gonna do? We're barely even scratching them.

Kenneth- I have one idea. We use our ultimate attacks. That might do it.

Crystal- It's worth a try.

The three warriors steady their breathing and take stances to use their ultimate attacks.

Kenneth- SOLAR FLARE STRIKE!!!!!!!!!!!!!!!!!!!!!

Crystal- SHOOTING STAR ARROW!!!!!!!!!!!!!!!!!

Tim- TSUNAMI STRIKE!!!!!!!!!!!!!!!!!!!!!!!!!

As the three use their ultimate attacks, the statues are sent across the room, and knocked to the ground.

Crystal (taking a deep breath)- It's about time they went down.

Tim (chuckling)- I'll agree with that.

Kenneth (grinning)- So will I, now let's get out of here and see if we can help Joseph and Kim with anything.

As the three turn and start to head for the exit of the room, they hear a noise coming from the direction of the stone statues.

Crystal (with disbelief in her voice)- You gotta be kidding me.

Tim- What is it gonna take to kill these things?

Kenneth (closing his eyes)- If we do it right, only one more attack.

Crystal (looking over at Kenneth)- What do you mean?

Kenneth- We have to focus all of our power and bring it to a focal point, and make ourselves into bombs. It's the only way to destroy those things.

Tim (looking at Kenneth in disbelief)- You're joking, right?

Kenneth (with acceptance in his voice)- No I'm not. There is no other way.

Crystal- Well I always wanted to go out with a bang, guess I'm gonna get my wish.

Tim (with acceptance in his voice)- Looks that way. Well let's do it.

Kenneth- Right. Joseph, Kim, I leave the rest to you, our friends. Alright, spread out, and start focusing you power, and when we've finished they'll be finished.

As the statues get to their feet and start moving towards the three warriors, the warriors start gathering their power and as they do their armor starts to glow white, and the more power they focus, the brighter their armor glows. As the statues draw closer, the warriors not only continue to focus their own power, but, draw on more power from around them, until suddenly, they charge the statues and leap into the air right in front of each statue, and as they do, all that is seen is a blinding white light, with a thunderous explosion. As the dust begins to settle, we find that the three statues have been completely destroyed, and the bodies of the three warriors can be found laying among the ruins of the statues.

Kim (slowing her pace and looking back as she hears the explosion)- What was that?

Joseph (sadness in his voice)- Our friends paying the ultimate price to help us. I won't let their sacrifice be in vain.

Joseph and Kim continue running down the hall that they used to leave their friends behind, and find Ryan to finish this ancient battle once and for all. As they continue down the hall, they see an open room, with a light shining from it. The two quicken their pace and within minutes are standing in the middle of the room. Looking around, they see giant pillars of ivory, with carving of past battles, and of past Black Shinobi Masters. As they continue their survey of the room, they see on one wall, a painting of a black dragon, and on the other wall, a painting of a Black Shinobi Master beheading what was thought to be the last of the White Shinobi Clan. Finally their eyes come to rest on a figure clad in black armor, sitting on a throne made of gold, flanked on either side by figures clad in black armor as well.

Ryan (raising his head to look at Joseph)- Well I must admit, I'm impressed. Because I'm so impressed by you, I'm gonna make you a onetime offer, join me and live, fight against me and I promise you will die. So what is your answer?

Joseph (looking directly into Ryan's eyes)- I'm afraid I'm gonna have to reject your offer, and I'm gonna have to kill you.

Ryan (looking down and shaking his head)- So unwise. Kill'em!

At Ryan's command his body guards leap into action, one leaping straight at Joseph, the other straight at Kim. As the two warriors jump away from each other and from Ryan's body guards, they each draw their swords and enter into the fray. Kim starts off her battle by racing in towards her enemy, and attempting to separate the upper half off his body from the lower half with a slash at his abdomen. The body guard showing surprising agility and control of his movement, stops his forward momentum and leaps backwards just in time to avoid Kim's attack. The body guard seeing a nearby pillar leaps at an angle at it so that his feet hit it first, and then pushes off and at Kim. As the body guard flies through the air at Kim, he unsheathes two short swords from his back with a reverse grip, and as he gets in close enough he attacks with the blades trying to remove Kim's head from her shoulders, luckily Kim brings both of her swords up in time to block his attack and as his feet touch the ground Kim buries her knee into his stomach, and follows it up with a back flip that she turns into an attack by kicking him squarely in the jaw and sending him to the ground. As Kim lands on her feet, she quickly reverses her grip on the sword she has in her left hand. As she finishes changing the grip she leaps into the air to come down on where her enemy should have been in an attempt to impale him on her blade, however, the bodyguard, seeing it coming managed to roll out of the way and after she lands, the body guard kicks her legs out from under her, sending her to the ground. The two combatants roll away from each other to put some space between them and then they each jump to their feet. As they get to their feet Kim seizes the advantage and attacks first by charging the body guard and using a horizontal slash across his stomach, and a vertical slash meant to cut him in half from head to groin, followed by a round kick to the head, and using the momentum created from the round kick, follows the kick up with another horizontal slash meant to remove his head from his shoulders. The body guard jumps back away from the first horizontal slash, parries the vertical slash, ducks under the round kick, and then blocks the final horizontal slash and follows it with a round kick of his own that connects with Kim's ribs, sending her flying through the air to hit the wall and crumple to the ground unceremoniously. The body guard seeing an opening dashes forward. As the bodyguard closes the distance he throws one of his short swords directly at Kim. Kim seeing the blade flying through the air deflects it with the sword in her right hand, sending it to land harmlessly on the ground in front of Ryan, and as the body guard closes the distance, he attempts to plunge his remaining sword through Kim's skull. Kim, seeing the attack coming, defends against it by slicing through the hand holding the sword and then she plunges her other sword straight through the body guards chest, impaling him and killing him instantly.

Meanwhile Joseph is facing a body guard that uses weapons that resemble nun-chucks with one major difference, his weapon has curved blades on the ends of it, making it a multi-purpose weapon. The body guard attacks first, swinging his modified nun-chucks in several vertical to horizontal combinations that Joseph can't block with his swords, so is forced to dodge the attacks. As Joseph sees the last attack of the combination he leaps in after it swinging one of his blades in a vertical attack meant to separate the bodyguard into to halves from head to groin, however, using the curved blade of one of the ends of his weapon the body guard blocks and parries the blow to the left before it can land and then counter attacks by attempting to slash Joseph across the chest from left to right, forcing Joseph to leap back and create some distance between the two warriors. The body guard lunges in twirling his weapon around his body and moving as if he is dancing causing Joseph to be pushed further back until his back is against the wall. Seeing that there is no where left to retreat to, Joseph leaps as high into the air as he can, braces his feet against the wall and then pushes off to fly over his enemies head to hit to the ground and using his left over momentum to go into a forward roll to bring him to his feet several feet from his enemy. Taking advantage of his enemy's back turned to him, Joseph races in and attacks with both swords slashing horizontally at his enemy's midsection, however, the body guard sensing the attack coming back flips over Joseph before he lands his attacks. As the body guard nears the ground, he kicks Joseph in his back sending him to the ground face first. As Joseph rolls to his back, he sees the body guard leap into the air above him, preparing to drive the curved blades of his weapon into Joseph's chest. Joseph seeing that the body guard has committed himself to this attack quickly rolls out of the way, and gets to his feet. As the body guard lands, Joseph strikes at his head as he turns to face him, and the body guard having made the mistake of committing himself to the attack that he did, has no way to defend against Joseph's strike. As Joseph turns away from the body guards falling, headless body, a short sword flies through the air plunging deep into Kim's chest. As Joseph sees this horrifying site, he races to catch Kim in his arms. As he slowly lowers her to the ground tears can be seen in his eyes.

Joseph (looking into Kim's eyes)- Don't you dare die on me.

Kim (in between gasps of breathe)- You are…. The one meant….. to go on from here….. not me.

Joseph (tears streaming down his face)- Stop talking damn it. Save your strength.

Kim (starting to bleed from her mouth and struggling to talk)- There is….. something I need….. to tell you (coughing before next sentence). I….. love….. you. Don't……let….. your…… anger….. consume you (Kim dies after this).

Joseph (still crying and holding her body close to him)- Kim, wake up. Don't die on me. NNNNNNNNOOOOOOOOOOOOOOOOOOOO OOOOOOOOOO!!!!!!!!!!!!!!!!

Ryan (walking from his throne)- If I couldn't have her, no one would.

Joseph (still cradling Kim's lifeless body and not looking at Ryan)- Shut up you bastard!!!!!!!!!!!!!!!!!

Ryan (laughing and continuing his slow walk from his throne)- Anger, good, let's see if you know how to use it.

Joseph (slowly lowering Kim's body the rest of the way to the ground then looking directly at Ryan)- You're a dead man. I'll cut you down for this.

With this, the final confrontation begins. Joseph rushes in at Ryan with a combination of a jab, a hook, and a round kick. Ryan blocks the jab and the hook, but, he ducks under the round kick causing Joseph to spin completely around, and as he gets face to face with Ryan again, Ryan connects with a thunderous uppercut that lefts Joseph into the air, and before he even hits the ground,

Ryan, follows it up with a round kick of his own sending Joseph to crash into a pillar and crumble to the ground. Joseph gets to his feet quickly and charges Ryan again, and as he nears him, he attacks with a rear hand punch that Ryan easily dodges, and then counters with jab and rear hand punch combination of his own to Joseph's head. Joseph quickly shakes the cobwebs from his head and gets back into the fight, attacking with a round kick with his left leg, that Ryan dodges, again, causing Joseph to spin completely around. Joseph, as he starts coming back to face Ryan, fakes a spinning heel kick and connects with the side of Ryan's head with a spinning back fist with his right hand. Seeing that Ryan is stunned momentarily from the attack Joseph follows it up with a jab, rear hand punch, and uppercut combination, that causes Ryan to stumble backwards a few steps. Seeing this, Joseph, launches a thunderous spinning heel kick with his right leg, sending Ryan spinning through the air to hit the ground hard. After the vicious kick launched by Joseph, Ryan slowly claims to his feet, touch his lower lip, and finding that Joseph has drawn his blood. After seeing the blood from his lip on his hand, Ryan reaches over his right shoulder to draw both of his swords and charges Joseph, attacking in a blind fury. Joseph unable to draw his swords before Ryan attacked ends up having to dodge all of the attacks that Ryan is throwing. After one double slash that Ryan attacks with that Joseph ducks under, Joseph launches a devastating uppercut, launching Ryan into the air, to land hard on his back. As Ryan climbs to his feet again, Joseph draws his swords. Seeing that Ryan is slow to get to his feet, Joseph charges him and attacks with a baseball like swing with the sword in his right hand, that Ryan quickly catches on the blade in his left hand knocking it out of the way and then retaliates with a vertical slash with the sword in his right hand. Joseph seeing the attack coming raises the sword in his left hand to catch the attack and then parry it to his left, and follows it with a raising diagonal slash meant to cut Ryan in half from left hip to right shoulder. Ryan, barely seeing the attack, leaps backwards *just in time to avoid a death stroke, but, his armor receives a long slash mark from the end of Joseph's sword.*

Ryan (looking at his scarred armor)- Impressive, you're the first to draw my blood and scar my armor in battle. I'll enjoy ending your life.

Joseph (looking directly at Ryan)- Shut up and fight you pompous bastard.

Ryan looks up from his armor at Joseph and smiles, then raises his swords while at the same time twists them so that his palms are facing upwards and combines his swords.

Ryan (smiling and looking directly at Joseph)- This is the end for you. DARK FLARE!!!!!!!!!!!!!!!!!!!!!

As Ryan leaps into the air, his blades change colors from the metallic silver to black as night. As Ryan starts his free fall, Joseph's armor and swords start to glow a brilliant white, and as Ryan nears him, Joseph brings both of his swords up in the form of an "x" and catches Ryan's attack on his blades.

Joseph (looking Ryan directly in the eyes as his facemask closes)- This battle is over. Now I will light this world's darkest hour and bring an end to your evil.

Joseph separates his swords, destroying Ryan's weapon.

Ryan(stunned disbelief)- No, this is impossible, I can't lose.

As Joseph separates his blades he brings them before him and combines them at the hilt.

Joseph (leaping into the air)- This is the end of you. ARMOR OF SHINOBI, FLARE UP NOW!!!!!!!!!!!!!!!!!!!!!

As Joseph comes down he slashes Ryan in half vertically, then spins around and slashes him in half horizontal, and continues the spin and separates his swords. Behind him, Ryan, is incinerated, and the extra power from his attack blasts every upper level of the Black Shinobi Temple into nothingness. As Joseph resheathes his blades, he notices that the extra power not only destroyed the temple, but, it also starts to return Virginia, and the world back to it's normal state.

Joseph (looking around)- It's over. The threat of the Black Shinobi Clan is over.

As Joseph starts to leave, he hears the sound of shifting rubble from the direction of where Kim's body was laying. Joseph cautiously goes over and starts to remove some of the debris and finds that Kim's body no longer has a sword in it, and even more amazing, she is moving. Seeing this, Joseph rushes to remove the rest of the debris, and as he clears the last of it, he squats down by her body and lifts her into his arms and as she comes to, tears start streaming down his face.

Kim (smiling up at him)- Hi.

Joseph (smiling as tears are rolling down his face)- Hi. How is this possible?

Kim (smiling and reaching up to touch his face)- I don't know, and I don't want to know. All that matters is that I'm here with you.

As Joseph helps Kim to her feet, Kenneth, Crystal, and Tim come into the room at a trot. As they come to a stop, Joseph can't help but to smile at each of them, and they in return the smile as well.

Joseph (looking and smiling at his friends)- It's over guys. Let's go home.

Kenneth (coming up and placing his hands on Joseph's shoulders)- I'll second that.

As the five leave and start to head for home, Joseph pulls Kim to the side.

Joseph (gazing into Kim's eyes)- I thought I lost you.

Kim (looking back into his)- You won't have to worry about losing me again for a long time, I promise.

Joseph (smiling at her)- Well, there is something I want to do that I should have done long ago.

Kim (giving him a smile in return)- And what's that?

Joseph (pulling her in closer to him)- This.

In that moment with the other three walking away, Joseph leans into Kim, closing his eyes, and kisses her. They stand there for several seconds locked in each other's embrace and kiss before separating and moving to join the other three, with Joseph wrapping an arm around Kim affectionately. Mean while in Hell, Ryan, in the midst of shifting from his human form to a demon form, makes a vow.

Ryan (raising a shifting fist)- I swear, one day, I will escape from here, and have my vengeance on you Joseph of the White Shinobi!!!!!!!!!

THE END

Printed in the United States
By Bookmasters